RABBIT PUNCHES

RABBIT PUNCHES

stories

JASON OCKERT

DZANC
BOOKS

DZANC BOOKS

5220 Dexter Ann Arbor Rd.
Ann Arbor, MI 48103
www.dzancbooks.org

ISBN: 978-1-950539-41-3
Dzanc edition: November 2021
First US edition April 2006, published by Low Fidelity press

Library of Congress Cataloging-in-Publication Data Available Upon Request

The following stories appeared previously and are reprinted by permission of the author: "Deviated Septum" in *Black Warrior Review*; "Adrift and Distant" in ReinventingTheWorld.com; "Shirtless Others" in *River City*; "Mother May I" in *McSweeney's*; "Des" in *CutBank*; "Scarecrowed" in *Virgin Fiction 2*; "Horseshoes" in *Knight Literary Journal* vol. 2; "Milkweed" in *Highway 14*.

Cover design: Steven Seighman

Printed in the United States of America

10   9   8   7   6   5   4   3   2   1

This is for Sharon, my mom, who walked with me every step of the way.

And this is for Dawn, who showed me how to soar.

Contents

To be, in the grass, in the peacefullest time,
Without that monument of cat,
The cat forgotten in the moon;

And to feel that the light is a rabbit-light,
In which everything is meant for you
And nothing need be explained

From "A Rabbit as King of the Ghosts"
Wallace Stevens

Infants and Men

Words change. Their meanings need to be updated all the time. Here at Causeway Dictionaries we change words. I have been working through the alphabet and am at the tail-end of *S* when my boss uses the house intercom to call me into his office. My office is downstairs, his is up. In the hallway, I hurry by my co-worker Bobb's office. Bobb's got a mean competitive side and I don't want him to know where I'm going. I hear his door open as I round the corner and take the stairs by twos.

This morning I discovered an inconsistency in the word *stroam*. *Stroam* means "to walk or stroll." I figure it should be changed to: "to stroll or *roam*." Stroll, roam; stroam. Right? I ask the boss.

No. Don't be so god-damned diaphanous, I know you've been fornicating with my wife, Mr. Causeway says. He hefts a Causeway Dictionary from his neat mahogany desk and propels it at me. Also on the desk is a wooden turtle I whittled for Mrs. Causeway a while ago. I don't know how it got there.

Mr. Causeway's an upstanding employer but he doesn't make much of a husband or father. Once he took

Bobb and me to the fringe of the bayou where we administered a prescribed burn. It was a company meeting of sorts. His dog Ray was there for the exercise. The wind blew a tuft of fur on the dog's head westward, which was right, so we lit the underbrush and watched fire eat duff around the Loblolly and such. We found well-worn stumps to sit upon and share whiskey. He told me a good fire unloosened him. He said at home he was outnumbered, even Ray was a bitch. I felt like protesting, but it didn't seem right to do at the time. He told us he was an entrepreneur, a hunter, a wordsmith, not a god-damned baby-sitter or love-maker. I looked up from whittling a chunk of Southern Oak with my four inch Tiger Blade and mentioned divorce. He shrugged his shoulders and changed the subject. Asked if I'd ever hewn anything of relevance.

I've made a few fine wooden frogs and I can build a decent tree-house, I answered.

He said, People devour adorable things. Downtown at the Knick Knack Shack patrons would just as soon buy fifty bulbed ornaments before procuring a pocket Causeway Dictionary.

Bobb concurred.

Maybe we could do business, Mr. Causeway said.

I'll see what I can manage, I assured him.

Meanwhile, how about building a structure for Chauncy in a Longleaf behind my abode?

I enjoy carpentry, too, Bobb said, but Mr. Causeway ignored him.

I was already humping Mrs. Causeway and this invitation seemed wonderful. Things happen like that sometimes; the saint holds the door for the sinner.

The fire petered out at the waterline, they polished

off the whiskey, Ray rested her muzzle in my crotch and I said, Sure, sure.

Now, in the office, I sidestep the book and try to explain.

I have enormous affection in my heart for her, I say.

That's part of the asses' bridge, he states, the fingertips of his big hands touching each other lightly. You're strutting around like a gilded rooster thinking what you got means more to her than just rutting. It don't.

Say whatever you want. You don't appreciate her the way I do.

Son, you're in deep. When did you drop down her rabbit hole?

I met her when I was your door-to-door dictionary salesman, I say.

That's what I used to do; door-to-door sales. I started in Ohio delivering newspapers. People referred to me as Paperboy. I didn't care for the term. One day, on a lunch break, I read a travel article about the antiquated values of the South. Although I didn't really understand what *antiquated* meant, I liked the sound of it. The article explained that the South was cut and dry; it didn't have boys, only infants and men. I wanted to be the latter. I didn't know how I was going to become a man, so I thought I should first be a Southerner. I made my way down to Mississippi, knocking on doors and pushing anything I could get hired to push from Kentucky Bourbon to Alabama Almonds. Then I arrived at Causeway Dictionaries.

Mrs. Causeway and I met one day when I tried to sell her one of her husband's dictionaries. I had a terrible pitch, it went: *Hi, I'm Deet! Bet you don't know what the word pusillanimous means!* Most people didn't and didn't care. Mrs. Causeway said, Darling, it means cowardly and you shouldn't go around using words like that. I blushed at her reprimand and low-cut blouse. She had on heels; I've come to know she always wears them. She noticed my skinned knuckles, skinned from rapping on doors. He is deplorable, she said, taking my hands and kissing my fingers, gazing at me from the top part of her eyes. Russet hair and a smell like cinnamon, my Mrs. Causeway.

The next day I brought her a wooden turtle, the same one that's sitting on Mr. Causeway's desk now. The turtle isn't my best work, but Mrs. Causeway found it endearing nonetheless. She led me out back to a pair of lawn chairs in the cranky St. Augustine grass. She sent Chauncy around the block, the long way, to walk Ray while we talked. She let me hold her hand. She told me to visit her when I could and I came day after day to hump regularly during my late lunch break. Little Chauncy would sit quietly downstairs and watch soap operas. Mrs. Causeway told me that I knew how to treat her like a lady, that I made her feel things she hadn't felt in years. She'd emit these contented sighs after a romp. My vocabulary sharpened and I developed sexual stamina. She said I made love with *perfervidium ingenium* and I knew exactly what she meant.

Now, in the office, Mr. Causeway cracks his knuckles. That'd be about three months you've been paunchy with my wife, huh?

Yes sir, I say, but I don't think you mean paunchy. Maybe pawky?

I'm giving you your mittimus, libertine, he responds.

I understand. Let me just pack my office up.

No. Go to the wife and apologize. You've been ungentlemanly. I spoke with her and she's waiting for you to address her. I'm disappointed in you, son. They've offered me two bucks for this wooden turtle at the Knick Knack Shack. I knew this blasted kitsch would catch on. Why couldn't you just whittle and leave the wife alone?

We're in love. I can't help that.

Don't make me get my rifle.

He keeps a rifle unloaded in the trunk of his green Corvette. He is the only one who would drive such a thing. There are bullets in the glove compartment. I haven't been hunting with him, but I've seen animals he's mounted in his guest room. I don't want to end up in there.

If you're threatening me, sir, perhaps we should get the police involved?

Mr. Causeway hoists another Causeway Dictionary and prepares to wing it at me when I sneak out the door.

Outside, broken clouds on the June skyline cannot determine which shade of rouge to wear into evening. I'm going to talk to Mrs. Causeway, ask her to run off with me. I should have done this two weeks ago, before our little spat. After I finished building the tree-house Mr. Causeway invited me over for dinner to celebrate. This was before he knew anything. He dominated the conversation with etymological trivia and hassled me about whittling wooden animals. Mrs. Causeway had her hair up and sat quietly with a stiff back. Chauncy mimicked her. The pork was over-cooked, we all noticed. Ray lapped water from her dish and watched me chew. Mr. Causeway suggested another drink after dinner. We'd been drinking since the fried okra hors d'oeuvres and

I didn't want the alcohol to trip my tongue so I excused myself.

The next day when I visited Mrs. Causeway she was tense and distracted. I tried to get her to open up with a joke about this midget I know from Kokomo, but she didn't find anything funny. She raked her nails down my back when we humped and drew blood. A splotch dripped onto the pillowcase and spread out like a little murder. Her apology was tight-lipped. I left awkwardly.

I stayed away for a while hoping she'd call. Then I couldn't remember if I had given her my phone number. I could have called her, but I figured phone conversation may not capture pivotal emotions and body language. Her syntax is beautiful but admittedly over my head often. That gave us room to grow. I want to ask her to grow with me. Wonder if I should propose; I could afford ring installments.

Out of the corner of my eye I see Bobb slinking behind a park bench. Bobb and I used to compete for the most sales when we were both door-to-door Causeway Dictionary salesmen. Then I got promoted to word-changer. Mr. Causeway gave me a raise because he noticed the improvement in my vocabulary. My vocabulary improved because I was trying to impress Mrs. Causeway. I studied the dictionary ravenously in my free time. But Bobb is still a door-to-door Causeway Dictionary salesman.

Bobb, I say, I see you, bastard.

Bobb looks like the little pink monster in the children's book I read to Chauncy. In the book, the monster is hidden somewhere on every page. He's tough to find. Bobb thinks of himself as a poet, an Italian poet. Sometimes he tries to push a dinky chapbook of poems at the door instead of dictionaries. As far as I know, judging by his last name, he is of French descent. He writes, *Night, and the jaded falcon beats its wings*, and other such cal. He is iambic. He wanted to trade poems and share thoughts with me. My poems aren't ready to share; certainly not with him. He wears enormous black-rimmed glasses and cannot walk without shuffling his feet.

Where are you off to, Deet? Bobb asks, grinning. He shuffles behind a sculpted fern.

That's none of your business.

Mr. Causeway find out about you and his wife?

I stare at Bobb. He stares back at me. We have a staring contest there, he half-hidden behind the hedge and me on the sidewalk. I wonder if he ratted me out. Probably, the fink. His eyes are holding steady. They are a milky brown. Mine are twitching and I don't know what color. They change from gray to greenish-blue depending on my outfit. Those glasses of his give him an unnecessary advantage, I think. He shifts his weight from foot to foot. My eyes are drying up. No way am I blinking, though. Birds overhead sing. The wind plays off my face threateningly. I start a mental chant, *Blink, Bobb, Blink*. He's probably chanting the same thing but with my name. I try to read his mind. It seems pretty simple; he thinks he is better than me. That's fine, what do I care? I shouldn't be here staring anyway. I've got Mrs. Causeway waiting for me at her home. I'll convince her that she and I and Chauncy should move to Florida and start over as a family. There are nice beaches in Florida, oranges and palm trees. I don't know if it's the South exactly, but we could figure that out together.

I blink.

Ha, Bobb says, pointing.

Did you tell our boss about me and Mrs. Causeway?

Maybe I did and maybe I didn't, Bobb says melodically.

God-damnit, you may have ruined a good thing.

Depends on how you look at it. With you gone, Mr. C will need to hire a new lexicographer. I'm his man. I know what se tirer d'affaire means, do you?

I chase Bobb about a block and let him scamper away through the kudzu. Bobb's quicker than me, my legs don't move like his.

The Causeways live in a semi-suburban neighborhood a half-mile from the office. They have the kind of house that is dwarfed by property. The backyard slopes down to a small forest and into the swamp. They have a problem with mosquitoes after a rain. The house has two stories with a basement. Mr. Causeway paid extra to have workers drain and construct the basement. He found it necessary for some reason. He keeps wine down there, but not enough to call it a wine cellar.

Knock-knock on the door and I am looking down at Chauncy. She is sipping from a fruit box. Hi, I say, and tweak her nose. Is your Mom around?

Hi Deet, she says smiling with punch-red lips. Her blonde hair is pig-tailed and she is wearing two cute blue bows which match her dress. Momma's up in the tree-house waiting for you, she says.

I'm glad someone's using it, I say.

Let me take you back. Chauncy grabs my hand and leads me around the house.

Chauncy makes a wonderful daughter. She is well-mannered and beautiful and smart. Sometimes she's precocious, but it only adds to her charm. Back when I was building the tree-house, Chauncy insisted on helping. I realized I'd have to build something over the bog to get to the Longleaf and Chauncy wanted to dig holes for the boardwalk posts. I bought her a small spade. She loved it and went around digging up the yard. Sometimes she'd make lemonade and we would sit in lawn chairs and chat. While she swung her legs in the lawn chair I'd clean the sap from my fingernails with my Tiger Blade. She told me she was afraid of heights and would never climb up into the tree-house but liked that I was building it anyway. She told me she liked me and hated her Daddy. She asked me to kill him for her.

Ha, I said, ha. Funny.

She didn't laugh back.

Hey, little girls aren't supposed to think like that, Chauncy. Mind yourself or I'll tell your Momma.

I'll tell her myself, Chauncy said and prepared to run inside.

No, no, don't bother. Why don't you sing to me while I build?

What do you want to hear?

Do you know the Chattanooga Choo-Choo?

She didn't, but I taught her.

Now Chauncy's humming *It's A Small World*. We round the house and she pulls me toward the boardwalk. I see Ray digging furiously at some wild mushrooms that have grown around a tree. Then I notice something that looks like a half-melted cherry Popsicle between her legs. I look closer and see that it is a small penis. I point this out to Chauncy.

What, his corny-dinger?

I thought Ray was a girl.

Nope, Chauncy says, he's a boy.

But he squats to pee.

He's a gentleman.

I suppose. The boardwalk ends at the Longleaf. Chauncy releases my hand and says, Good luck.

What do you think of Florida? I ask her.

Mickey Mouse is for babies.

True. What about Georgia?

Momma gets peaches from there.

Exactly.

I'm going to dig a hole for you.

That's nice. We can plant a tree.

Chauncy runs down the boardwalk toward the house. Her receding footsteps on the wooden planks sound like promises. I step lightly on the bottom split two-by-four spiked into the Longleaf and climb.

Mrs. Causeway is older than me by twenty years, has a fine accent, knows how to apply make-up. She is sitting with her legs tucked under her arms. She is wearing a long red dress and her high heels have been removed and rest next to a glass of Chardonnay by her side. Her toenails are painted.

You look like a rose bud, love, I say when I am up top with her.

The sky is full of uncomfortable air, sticky somehow. Evening brings cricket banter. There is a perfectly symmetrical spider web in the branches above us, but I don't see the spider.

Dear, don't be so platitudinous, Mrs. Causeway says, stretching her legs out in front of her. I am nothing like a rose bud.

You're right. We need to be doughty now that we are sequestered, I say.

No, we aren't, she says.

I look beneath us and see nobody.

She motions toward the bog. I see Bobb. The last of the day's sunlight glints off his glasses as he darts behind Spanish moss.

Who is he? She asks.

A son-of-a-bitch, forget him. I can't get you off of my mind, I'm not sore about the other day.

That man shouldn't be here.

Don't worry about him. He works for your husband.

Where's Chauncy?

Digging, I guess. Hey Bobb, I shout, we see you. Don't make me come down there and kick your ass.

Bobb disappears.

I flex my biceps and nod. See, he's gone.

Deet, we need talk. People change. You've got a lot of growing...

I know, I know, we can grow together. We can work this out. I believe in us. I've been writing poetry about you. I'd like to read it to you on the beaches of Florida or maybe in a peach tree grove in Georgia. We'll grab Chauncy and go. I'd make a good step-father to her.

It's valid that Chauncy has developed an affinity for your rambunctiousness. You'd make a fine playmate if you were neutered. She could use a friend.

Exactly, love. I touch her knee.

Mrs. Causeway pulls her legs back to her body and holds them. She says, But you haven't been paying attention to what's going on around here.

This is somewhat confusing.

I mean, my discountenance should have been felt by my actions.

What actions?

I over-cooked the pork, I lacerated your back.

I got over that, I can't stay away.

That's part of your downfall. Can't you understand that you're still an adolescent chanticleer?

That doesn't sound good.

It means a boy with a nice body.

My heart, just like that, is sand-papered, and I can feel it in my eyes.

Deet, look at me. She touches my jaw with the back of her hand and despite her reproaches I'm grateful for the contact.

I told my husband about us, she whispers.

I turn my head away and dangle my legs over the edge of the tree-house. I start to swing them but realize this is childish so I settle. Something is caught in my throat; it feels like Michigan.

Aren't you a little in love? I manage.

No.

Your husband is so callous.

I know, he'll get his. She pauses and stares into the tree limbs above.

I'm not sure what she means, but I'd do just about anything for us. She can be curt at times, like now, but I think she's just misunderstood. At root, she's as kind as can be. She has a spontaneous laugh that took me two weeks to earn. But when I did, it sprang out from her chest like a sparrow. So sweet and honest. She opened up and I tried to treat her as gently as I could. I want to tell her that I can be patient. I know that she is caged with her husband, that she is frightened of the future, and that's natural, however, can't you see our hearts palpitate as one? Before I can say this though, I am distracted by Ray baying below. The mutt is tapping up and down the boardwalk and, in the dying light, looks golden.

Chauncy skips along behind the mutt, pirouetting with spade in hand.

When are you coming down? Chauncy calls up to us.

Soon, dear, Mrs. Causeway says. Run along now.

I see Bobb reappear behind the moss with a pad of paper and pen. He is taking notes. I should scream at him again, but I don't want to agitate Mrs. Causeway any further.

Chauncy starts to sing, *Engine, engine, number nine, going down Chicago line, if the train falls off the track*, as she starts to skip away.

I turn to Mrs. Causeway, deciding in the moment I'm ready to act like the man I left the Midwest to become.

Marry me? I ask.

But when I turn, I see that Mrs. Causeway has scooted up behind me and is poised with her legs reared back. Then she solidly kicks me and I am falling and falling headlong.

Do you want your money back? I hear Chauncy ask.

I do, I do.

In Heaven there's a deer head and an alligator head and a big swordfish and a little girl who says her name is Chauncy. She is so soft and tells me it's a miracle I'm alive and Bobb was there to provide mouth-to-mouth though I think it's no big deal, I'm just Deet lying on the bed thinking angel Chauncy sure is pretty standing over me with her hair in a rope I'd like to climb if my arms worked better than they do. My arms lift some, I lift them, and darling Chauncy thinks I want a hug so she leans in and maybe that is what I want because it feels nice that she is close and loves me.

I'll protect you, Deet, Chauncy says. Momma's going to get you a wheelchair and won't that be nice to go on walks?

I nod my head because my head nods and it would be nice to go out sometime and go for a walk with angel Chauncy.

Let me check something, Chauncy says, and she unzips my pants and yanks them down and thumps my corny-dinger a few times and says, Daddy's gonna be happy that doesn't work anymore, and she laughs and I laugh too but have to pee so I stop.

When the wheelchair comes I'm strong enough to sit up in it and darling Chauncy pushes me around, though she has trouble getting me through doorjambs, but we manage and she walks me everywhere and some people say Hi, Deet, we were worried about you, and I wave and Chauncy tells me to tell them I'm doing just fine and will be better in no time so I say, I'm doing just fine in time even when they don't ask so Chauncy flicks my ear and tells me to only say it when someone asks, How are you doing, Deet? And then I say, I'm doing just fine and better.

Soon angel Chauncy wheels me to the place she says her Daddy works. We go up-up in an elevator and then we are in front of a door and I can hear people talking on the other side. I don't want that infantile invalid in my guest room anymore. His spittle has stained my Nana's down comforter, someone behind the door says.

Sir, I hear another man say, you probably don't want him to go to the hospital. They might suspect that Mrs. Causeway pushed him from the tree-house on purpose.

Wasn't it self-defense?

Hard to say, sir.

Well if anyone asks it shouldn't be hard for you to say it was an accident. Anyway, I'm not taking him to the hospital. If I did he wouldn't be able to manufacture these trinkets.

If I'm not imposing, might I suggest you put him in the basement until he regains some of his faculties?

And then Chauncy knock-knocks on the door and the men inside go quiet and she squeezes me into the room.

Hi, Deet, a man in a chair says to me.

I don't say anything. Then Chauncy whispers that this is her Daddy and to call him Mr. Causeway so then I say, Hi, Mr. Causeway.

You remember Bobb, don't you, Mr. Causeway asks and he turns his eyes to the other man who is standing with arms behind his back and is smiling wide-wide and must be so happy. He has on big glasses that look funny.

I shake my head, No, because I don't remember Bobb at all.

That's fine, Mr. Causeway says. Bobb, will you excuse us, please?

Certainly, the man in the glasses replies and as he is walking out of the room he steps on my foot and says he's sorry but I didn't feel it and it didn't hurt. Chauncy closes the door behind him and Mr. Causeway holds up a wooden turtle.

Do you remember this? Mr. Causeway asks.

I shrug my shoulders.

Then Mr. Causeway takes a chunk of wood out of a drawer and a mean looking knife and slides them across the desk and Chauncy puts them in my lap where they sit there. Then I feel drool on my chin and want to wipe it off but at the same time I know I should concentrate because Mr. Causeway has a face that tells me to behave.

Pick up the blade and see what you can do, he says as he touches his fingertips together.

I pick the knife up and hold it in front of me for a long time.

Whittle, damn you, he says.

I try to blow sound out of my lips but just drool more and he gets all red like he is hot.

Whittle, Deet, not whistle. Remember, little animals, ducks, turtles, frogs, you know.

And though I don't know, I shake my head Yes, and wipe my chin on my shirt and feel like crying.

Daddy, dear Chauncy says, I'll teach him.

He's going to earn his keep, Mr. Causeway says sternly.

And dear Chauncy opens the door and wheels me out of the building to the outside and I can't help thinking about what Mr. Causeway said and I don't want the knife in my lap and so I say, I don't want to hurt little animals.

No, darling Chauncy says, don't worry about that right now. Give me the knife.

And so I don't worry and I give her the knife and she pushes me home to rest.

Later when I wake up I see the deer head and the alligator head and the swordfish and Chauncy staring down at me with narrow eyes. Only now Chauncy is much, much older and with make-up and free hair.

Hello, Deet, she says, and I realize that her voice is different and this isn't angel Chauncy at all. She asks, How are you doing?

And I remember what little Chauncy told me and so I say, I'm doing just fine and I will be better in no time.

That's good, dear. How is your strength?

I don't know, so I lift my arms as much as I can and she doesn't hug me and instead raises her voice and says, Higher, higher. I struggle and lift them up and almost to her chin.

Work on that, she says and leaves. I work and work until my muscles are sore.

Sweet Chauncy takes me on a walk to the swamp and props a shovel under my arm so it looks like I've got a lance and am charging. We go over a boardwalk and through trees and out to the swamp and it is rough riding. Big mosquitoes bite my arms and leave boob-marks, that's what Chauncy calls them, and she tells me to use my fingernails and put an x on the spot to make it feel better which I do.

We are singing *Here we go round the prickly pear, the prickly pear, the prickly pear* when I see a big hole and I think Chauncy is going to roll me in but she stops at the edge and says, We're here. She takes the shovel, climbs in the hole and digs.

I ask, Whatcha digging for, Chauncy?

She says nothing and throws a pile of wet dirt on my head and I laugh because it's funny but she has a tight face on so I stop and hate her for a while.

But Chauncy is a great girl and she knows I'm mad at her and when she's wheeling me home she says, It's a hole for my Daddy.

Ha, I say, ha, because I think this is funny and Chauncy laughs too and everything is fine.

Back home the man with the big glasses is dragging wood into the basement. Chauncy leaves me in the living room and takes the dog Ray on a walk around the block. I sit and watch the man drag more and more wood down there and ask, Whatcha doing?

The man stops and adjusts his glasses and walks over to me and stares. I try to look away but his eyes follow me around.

He leans down low and says, You've got some serious cobwebs up there, don't you buddy, and he raps his knuckles on my head.

My brain starts to pound so I smack him in the face.

He is surprised and pulls his hand back to hit me when we both hear high heels clicking in the hallway and the bigger Chauncy is there and I learn this is Mrs. Causeway because the man with the glasses acts like he is stretching and says, Mrs. Causeway, don't you look lovely today?

Thank you, Bobb, Mrs. Causeway says. How is the ramp coming?

Excellently, Bobb says, I should be finished tomorrow.

Superb, Mrs. Causeway says as she gets behind my wheelchair. She shoves me into my room and slams the door. I hear hammering and sawing down below as I struggle to get out of the chair and into the bed.

All the next day I hear hammering and sawing and in the meantime I lift my arms up again and again and stretch for the ceiling. I talk to the animal heads mounted on the wall even though I realize they're not alive and won't talk back. When I drool, I wipe the drool on my sheets. When I need to pee, I pee. When the hammering and sawing stops I keep right on lifting my arms.

Finally, the sun quits peeking in my window which means it is almost night so I try to go to sleep. Then the door opens and I am excited thinking Chauncy has come to play. But it is not Chauncy, it is Mr. Causeway who stomps in and brings with him a scent I know, the sweet smell of whiskey.

What in Hell's that stink? Mr. Causeway demands. Before I can answer he lifts the blanket and shouts, You've soiled my Nana's bed sheets, haven't you?

I try to answer the first question so I can answer the second one, but I can't because he lifts me up by my shirt front and tosses me to the ground. I bump the wall and the swordfish tilts over and nearly falls down on me. Then I see angel Chauncy at the door.

Leave him alone, Chauncy says.

Mr. Causeway shoves her against the other wall where the deer head is mounted and it tips but doesn't fall and little Chauncy closes her eyes to rest although I know the bang she suffered must have hurt. While Mr. Causeway isn't looking I crawl over to his leg and bite him. He howls and kicks me and then I see Mrs. Causeway in the doorway demanding that he stop which he does but only so he can hit her. I do what I can to get into my chair. When I'm nearly in, Mr. Causeway hustles me out of the room forcing Mrs. Causeway to jump aside and it is all I can do to hang on. Mr. Causeway takes me to the basement door and I see that there is a ramp built up next to the staircase and I am suddenly soaring down. I do not go very far when I find out that the ramp hasn't been built completely and it stops before I get to the bottom so I go flying out of my chair with my arms forward and I skid on the concrete and crash against a wall of bottles. One bottle falls and cracks next to my head and spills sweet red wine under me. Over my shoulder I see Mr. Causeway staggering down the stairs.

I'm going to get my money out of you, god-damnit. Where did you put that knife?

And I know that I gave the knife to Chauncy and am going to answer him when I notice Mrs. Causeway at the top of the stairs and I see that she has the knife, not Chauncy, and it is raised over her head as she scurries behind Mr. Causeway and buries the blade in his neck. And Mr. Causeway is surprised by this because his eyes widen and he turns around and walks back up the stairs, gurgling, with one arm forward and the other at his neck and soon he is standing where Mrs. Causeway was standing and then out of my sight.

I set my face in the wine and my head starts to spin so I close my eyes for a while.

When I open them it is dark. I hear Ray sniffing in my ear. He licks my face and then laps at the wine. It's hard for me to remember where I am and what happened. Then, there in the pitch black, it occurs to me that the sensation of hurling out of my chair to the basement floor is familiar; I recall that I've fallen before.

By the time it is morning I have righted my chair and am sitting in it. I watch a spider crawl around the room, up my leg, and onto my knee. I don't feel it there, but I crush it all the same.

Eventually dear Chauncy bounds down the stairs and says, Good morning. She has a bright yellow Band-Aid on her forehead which matches her dress. Her hands are behind her back because she has a surprise.

Good morning, I say.

Deet, she says, things have changed some. You and I are going to play in the basement for a while. I'm going to teach you how to whittle. She brings her hands from behind her back and holds out the knife to me, handle-first. Here's your knife back, she says, and thrusts it forward, and I don't want it but darling Chauncy is firm this morning and I have no choice.

How do I whittle? I ask.

You'll see. I'll go get some soft wood for you to work on. She takes the stairs by two on her way up.

The knife feels heavy in my hands and it flips up. It is mostly clean, but I can see some dried blood down inside the groove and I remember Mr. Causeway and what he said about killing turtles and small animals and I don't want to so I throw the knife at the water heater.

Dear Chauncy comes back down with some wooden blocks and she sees the knife on the floor.

What's this? she asks.

I blush and turn my head away from her because she has her hands on her hips and I am in trouble, but I can be strong too and I tell her that I will not kill any animals.

And angel Chauncy is a great girl so she laughs and calls me silly and picks up the knife and dances with it. We spend the day with her helping my hand move the blade across the wood and carve it. When night comes my fingers are tired and my lap is full of woody-shavings.

Now, it's important that you learn how to do something worthwhile, that's why you're learning how to whittle, Chauncy says. Momma wants you to keep the knife by your side because it's yours. She's not going to let you come up out of the basement until you know how to carve wooden animals. You should do what Momma says.

I nod.

I know my Daddy did some rotten things last night, but don't you worry about that now. Momma told me you stabbed him good.

But I didn't…

Now, now, don't be afraid, nobody's going to tell. Momma's going to work where Daddy used to work changing words around. She's just as good as he was. Momma will smooth things over, you hear?

I am quiet for a minute and then say, Yes.

Good.

Does your forehead hurt?

Chauncy lightly touches her Band-Aid. Nope, it doesn't. Sometimes you have to be strong if you're a woman.

I tell her I like women and she says, Good. I ask her where I'm supposed to go to the bathroom and she brings me a pink pan and helps me undo my pants.

I spend a lot of time down in the basement carving wood blocks. I make a seal. Chauncy can't tell that it's a seal so I make a dog using Ray as a model. Even though Chauncy says that my wooden dog looks more like a wolf she decides to push me up out of the basement.

I am happy to be above ground and it is evening again and Mrs. Causeway is in the kitchen cooking something and Ray has his muzzle in my lap. Angel Chauncy and I are in the living room putting together a puzzle. I'm not much help with the puzzle which is going to look like the picture on the box which is of a big rainbow-colored tree.

There is a knock-knock on the door, right behind us. Chauncy is about to fit a piece into the puzzle but stops right there and watches Mrs. Causeway wipe her hands on a dish rag and adjust her breasts first the right and then the left. As she comes out of the kitchen I hear that she is wearing high-heels and the sound of them seems to come after she has already walked by us to the door.

And at the door is the man with the glasses who I remember is Bobb. He is holding roses which he gives to Mrs. Causeway who ohh's and takes him by the hand. He closes the door and lets her lead him up the stairs where I know Mrs. Causeway has her bedroom. Bobb shuffles his feet and looks at me like I'm responsible for something awful but he is kind of smiling at the same time. I'm feeling dizzy staring at his glasses because I can't see his eyes too good, so I shut my lids and hold my breath and count, *one, two, three*; I know who Bobb is, I've seen him before, maybe in a children's book I used to read?, *four, five, six*. My breath wants out so I release it and look and Bobb is gone.

Who's that? I ask Chauncy.

She fits the puzzle piece and says, Bobb.

I know his name is Bobb, but who is he?

Chauncy narrows her eyes like I've seen Mrs. Causeway do, and she thinks for a moment. Then she leans over the table and gets close to my ear and whispers, her hot breath spreads over my face like sweet cinnamon and I feel my corny-dinger tingle and stand a little bit, enough to make Ray raise his head, which means maybe I'm getting better, and she whispers, That there's a rabbit Momma's gonna eat up.

Deviated Septum

Alston Goldstein rides on his yellow moped which has a basket between the handlebars where he normally keeps drugs but which today has a black mask and butterscotch candies in it. When Alston tried the mask on this morning at the Margate Swap Shop he decided he looked like Casanova. It forms a dark band around his head with oval holes for eyes. Those who saw him trying it on regarded him as a skinny blonde-redheaded Zorro too old to be purchasing a mask this time of year. It is not Halloween or near Halloween.

When Alston fishes into the basket for the butterscotch candies there is a delicate moment as he negotiates the graveled Interstate-95 median with one hand. Heavy trucks in passing could tip him. But Alston is undaunted, heading, with a slight flurry of butterflies in his stomach, toward the Wyngate retirement community. The wind and traffic have stifled the sound of his perpetual nose-whistle and Alston can concentrate on chomping his candy and having sex. Alston has not had sex, though he is eighteen and has thought about it. At the pharmacy, there are magazines that slip out of brown covers and reveal intercourse. Alston has used these as guides. He has understood himself in his father's bathroom, at Goldstein's Pharmacy, with a magazine or two. Masturbating is wrong; Alston learned this from his father. He puts the magazines back in their brown containers convinced he is done with the whole affair each time.

Louisiana Harrison, who moved to South Florida years ago, goes by Izzy. Louisiana is too long for a name so she shortened it. She liked the way a man said Izzy; it rumbled up out of him like a growl. She draws a bath and disrobes. The cold water isn't working well this morning. Numbness in the left side of her jaw causes her mouth to dip slightly in a frown. She ignores the lack of feeling and moves to the kitchen to turn on her radio as the tub fills. Izzy likes big-band; it plays from a transistor radio next to the stove. She takes two steps backward and one step forward, spins in a slow circle, her body wrinkled and fair and worn. Shuffling into the bathroom where the bath is ready, she turns the water off, but it drips indignantly. As she bends and steps into the too-hot water she has a stroke and collapses. Water splashes onto a faded green rug. Convulsions throw an arm over the side of the tub, her head slumps with her mouth resting on her chest a few inches from the water. She breathes raggedly out of her nose. Big-band drifts faintly into the bathroom but Izzy doesn't hear this. She is in a catatonic dream state consisting of half-realized notions of her home in Louisiana. She hears blues, but it is mostly just a low bass riff moving up and down scales, like a dripping faucet, or the beating of an old heart under water. She smells bananas in heavy air. She's on a porch with a fan and a hat and a drink and thinks, *How lovely,* and, *how lovely it would be to dance, even in this heat, slowly, with a man.*

At the Margate Swap Shop, Alston asked about the elephant. He asked the blond man with big jowls and sweat in the rolls of his neck behind the register.

The man said it was killed. He also said the mask was five-fifty.

Alston had the money; he'd earned it by delivering medication to the elderly every other day. The mask was worth it, he felt, he looked good, mysterious. He asked how they killed the elephant.

The man didn't know. A swarm of gnats descended upon him.

A young woman tapped Alston on the shoulder and twirled her curly hair with a finger. She had been eavesdropping at the Margate Swap Shop for five years, since she'd married too early and succumbed to a rut of profound boredom. Her husband was a cop, she didn't understand his duties, but he knew about the incident. She mentioned to Alston that she overheard their conversation about the elephant.

Alston clutched the bag tightly in his fists. The heat, the idea of having neck rolls like the blond cashier, and this woman, who was the same height as Alston and had a seductive fuzzy upper-lip, made his palms hot and his nose whistle. He said, Yes, we were chatting about the elephant tragedy. Upon saying this Alston felt he sounded inauthentic. Chatting is a word hard on the teeth.

The woman thought the boy had a sort of European charm with his reddish hair and all. She said; They shot the elephant with a big gun.

Alston shifted his weight. He figured this is what they had done, popped the elephant. He had wanted to say to Izzy, who had shown him the elephant article a few days earlier, I bet they popped the elephant. But he had not said this because it wasn't the point at all. Now, however, to this woman beneath the tarp at the Swap Shop, Alston could make his point, which was: The elephant was just being an elephant.

It killed a mother and her baby, the woman responded.

I know, I'm sorry, really, believe me, I feel, but you can't blame the elephant.

The woman, who on occasion took men from the Swap Shop to a Comfort Inn down the block for miniature affairs, thought the boy could be fun to ravage if he kept his mouth shut and controlled his nose-whistle. He could be kinky with his mask. Maybe he was beyond his years. She asked: Who else can you blame?

Alston was getting lightheaded beneath the canopy in the South Florida heat, trying to think this through. He said, his voice cracking slightly, If you need to blame somebody blame God or fate or this ridiculous heat or animal trainers or something. The elephant had had enough, it ran, it trampled a couple of tourists, I'm sorry, it tried to escape through the parking lot, I hear it damaged a Mercedes, I think its name was Chloe.

The woman put her hand on Alston's shoulder. You really care about the elephant don't you, baby?

Alston felt intimidated by the woman's arm; it had a surprising heft. It's not that I care too much, I just think I can understand more how the elephant felt than the tourists. I was born here but I don't like it. I want to know what they did with the carcass.

Why? the woman asked. She massaged Alston's shoulder and breathed on his face.

Because maybe it escaped after all, beyond this life, laid to rest, sent to Africa to some elephant cemetery, I don't know.

The woman noticed she had a chipped nail. That's too much work. They'll probably put it in a museum, but I don't care.

Alston tried to step out of the woman's grip. This woman was nothing like the women in the magazines, she was forceful, cunning, clothed. The magazine women were eager to please. Will they stuff it for the museum, and what do you stuff an elephant with? Is it relegated to an air-conditioned tomb? Will they put some information on an index card stating that elephants can be dangerous and to avoid them at Swap Shops if they get to running? Is the trunk going to wither...

Let's take your mask and go up the road.

Alston took a deep breath and remembered the mask. His nose whistled. I have to go now, he said, straightening his back. My name is Gold, perhaps I'll see you again, thank you for the information. He gently took her hand off his shoulder.

The woman noticed that the boy's voice had gotten deeper and he tried to speak with a Southern accent. She acknowledged her desperation in a lucid instant and made a mental note to: never have children, understand or leave her husband, stop swap shopping, go to the beach and have tourists bury her under the sand.

Izzy decides to go swimming at the country-club pool in Baton Rouge. She knows people there, people would like to see her. The water is perfect, tepid and nice. She swims slowly on her back in a light-colored bikini. Men on lounge chairs admire her with slight smiles. She hears a brave man dive into the deep end to swim near her. A water-bird passes overhead making lazy strokes in the wind. The rustling water in her ears sounds like compliments.

On Tuesday when Alston delivered medication to Izzy, she pointed to a newspaper and said, Look at this.

Alston had finished taking out the trash and emptying the ashtrays which he did for Izzy. He also organized her bookshelves, ate her cookies, listened to her music, and chatted with her into the evening. She was the last stop on his route and he could afford her the time. He wanted to do things for her because she was patient and understanding. She never said anything about his nose-whistle and there were times with her when he forgot about it. He enjoyed her Southern accent, the stories of her youth, and the tilt of her head when she walked. She had a way of incidentally touching Alston's hand that made him feel a part of her history. He spied black-and-white pictures of her in an album she kept under her coffee table while she was in the bathroom; she had been a zinger. In one she wore a bathing suit and the smile on her face had warmth that defied the worn edges of the picture. When Izzy returned to the living room that image lingered, Alston saw the similarities between her now and what she had been in her soft-blue eyes.

The other elderly were cretins. They had bruised skin and voices like crickets. Alston was distinctly aware that his nose-whistle sounded like them. They hated to see him when he appeared with his white paper bags beyond their screened doors, mosquitoes rising from the tall grass to bother his elbows. They thought, *This then will be it for me*, struggling from tan armchairs dead-center in front of old televisions, *this then, this boy with his bag of tricks*.

Izzy pointed a wrinkled finger at the newspaper and Alston had read the headline, "Mother and Baby Trampled by Renegade Elephant." He read the article and said, Wonder what the elephant was thinking?

Izzy snorted and said, Not that, this, and she pointed her finger again. Earlier in the day Izzy had suffered one of the two mini-strokes she would have before Friday morning. It was just a quick burning in her throat like too-hot coffee going down the wrong tube. Her vision blurred and her jaw began to numb. She noticed these things but was not overly concerned. She would mention it to her doctor on Saturday.

Alston read a two-paragraph piece about a bandit breaking into elderly homes, taking one valuable item such as a bracelet or necklace, and saying "I will remember you eternally," with a sad British accent. In a couple of cases, the article announced, the bandit had taken the hand of the female victim and kissed it.

What do you think? Izzy had asked, slurring her words a bit.

He sounds cartoonish.

He's handsome.

I don't think you mean handsome, they didn't say what he looked like, just masked.

I can see him well enough, Izzy said. He's tall with silver hair, all dressed in black with green eyes and a solid chin. His Southern accent finds a secret somewhere inside you and stays deep there.

The article said he had a British accent.

Never mind the particulars, Alston. You don't know. I feel passion. I feel heat. Izzy's eyes filled with tears. She didn't know why she felt sad exactly, she didn't think she should. The mini-stroke had twisted her emotions. Without a doubt she wanted an action to occur in her life.

I would eat a man like that right up, Izzy said.

She turned her head to gaze out the window. A strand of white hair brushed her cheek. She crossed her pale legs. She parted her lips and drummed her fingernails against her teeth.

As Izzy imagined seducing the bandit in the kitchen, against the refrigerator or over the stove so that the circular burner pressed into her flesh, Alston felt the heat from his face creep down into his lap.

Izzy steps from the pool and towels off. Clouds hold rain in the thick, humid air. She runs her fingers through her damp hair and toys with a few of the pursuing gazes from gentlemen in lounge chairs. *There*, she thinks, *there, I'll take that one there.* She studies his approach with his shoulders thrown back, chest forward. Drumming her nails on her teeth, she sizes him up: *Solid chin, green eyes, manicured black hair. Let me hear him speak.*

On Thursday, Alston brought a bag of grapefruit to Izzy. The front door was slightly open. When he pushed into the apartment he saw her sitting at the kitchen counter smoking a cigarette, in makeup. She turned toward the door with an excited look of expectation that fell flat when she saw Alston.

Were you expecting someone else?

Yes.

I brought some grapefruit.

Izzy smiled weakly, her lip frustrated.

Is something wrong?

An ashtray on the counter smoldered. Izzy had been crying earlier but now she was angry. Another mini-stroke had made her shoulder stiff. Big-band played from the radio.

I feel fine, Alston, just not in the mood to chat today, honey.

Alston set the grapefruit on the counter. I'm not a child, he said, I can feel too.

You are a child, your feelings are narrow.

Alston hadn't heard Izzy this way. Since Tuesday he had been denying the thoughts he had about her. He bought the grapefruit because it is something he would give his own grandmother. Izzy could accept the fruit and establish her role as elderly sweetheart again.

Why are they narrow?

You haven't lost anything.

Alston thought of the elephant from the Swap Shop. That was a loss, somehow, but it seemed feeble to try to explain this to her.

Look, Izzy, I can only be what I am.

Exactly, honey.

What should I do?

Age.

Why don't you have a grapefruit, I'll peel it for you.

I'm not hungry for that.

It starts to rain as Izzy and the gentleman caller stroll to her estate arm-in-arm. He tries to cover her head and neck with a towel, which doesn't help. They laugh and sprint playfully up the lawn. Izzy's legs are strong and unencumbered in her bathing suit; teacup white. The gentleman caller follows at a few paces encouraging Izzy to keep running, *I'm just behind you*. The green towel falls to the trim grass in a heap, forgotten.

On his moped, now, Friday at dusk, battered by wind, Alston munches his butterscotch candies. He has recently changed his name from Alston Goldstein to Gold, Alston Gold, as part of his motif. He will explain to his father that Gold demands priority. He is saving the gold wrappers from the candy. His shoelaces are golden and he has a gold necklace with the Star of David on it. Everything else he wears is black.

Ahead of Alston, advancing at his pace, half in the median, a construction truck lumbers. There is a blue tarp whipping out of the bed and lashing the wind. It occurs to Alston that the elephant carcass could fit in a truck this size. If they didn't send it back to Africa maybe they carried it in a truck like this one out of Florida and buried it in a cold and generous pit up North. Alston figures the elephant was either running toward the beach, instinctively toward another continent, or north just to get away. That's where the body ought to be.

The old guard at Wyngate, who has not fought in any wars and holds a grudge, stops Alston.

We don't get you today, the guard says.

Special delivery for Flo LeMont, she has something wrong with her chest.

The guard calls Flo: Yeah, sorry to bother you. Alston, the boy with the drugs, is here to see you. Yeah, you have something wrong with your chest. The boy with the drugs. I'm the guard. No, the boy has the drugs, I'm the guard. I feel fine. I'm sending him to you. He'll knock on the door. Turn the television down. Take the medication the boy brings, it is for your chest. I don't know, ask him how many. Take them with orange juice. Until the pain stops. No, your husband is gone. Good-bye now, Flo.

Flo has Alzheimer's and won't miss Alston. He directs his moped through the narrow Wyngate streets, past the golf course with a family of dirty ducks and over yellow speed-bumps. The sun is all but gone, eaten by the Everglades. Alston parks behind a palmetto tree next to Izzy's apartment.

Izzy and her gentleman caller sip hot tea on her front porch. The gentleman caller sits on a lacquered rocking chair across from Izzy. They comment on the rain and exchange furtive glances. The rain carries a slight chill that the tea can't quite reach. A lazy fan spins above. Izzy can't control a shiver the gentleman caller notices. He stops his rocking and stands.

As Alston expected, the door is unlocked. He puts the mask on quickly before stepping inside the apartment. She isn't in the living room. This gives Alston time to gather his thoughts. He thinks about stealing a quick peek at the photo album for reassurance, but there isn't time for that. It is important that he breathe through his mouth in order to stifle the nose-whistle. Izzy would recognize the whistle. Alston's father explained the deviated septum when he believed Alston was man enough to understand, a couple of years ago, on Alston's sixteenth birthday.

You were born with it, son, it's called a deviated septum, you will always have that wheeze. Live with it, his father had said, it'll make you stronger.

How? Alston asked.

You'll be put down, people will look at you funny, you'll grow.

I don't want that.

Your mother and I bought you a moped, buck up, it's in the driveway.

Alston wasn't satisfied by this explanation. The deviated part bothered him. If he was deviated in the nose, what about his arms, his legs, his head, his heart?

The gentleman caller takes Izzy's hands and she stands. She sets the tea on a side table and glides with music from inside, across the porch. Slow blues from a phonograph in the living room escapes out the windows to explore the air. She dips her shoulders and spins in a pirouette, the rain slips in and wets her calves.

The periphery of his eyesight catches the black edges of the mask and makes Alston feel trapped. He can almost taste the smoked cigarettes lingering in the room. When he sees Izzy, he will act decisively. He will say, in a low Southern accent, something like, *I have traveled far and wide to be with you, angel.* The angel part was crucial, it seems right to call her that, *angel.* If he has to, Alston will say more, put her at ease. He figures they could drift into the bedroom to the bed. They'd simply take off their clothes and pieces would fit together neatly.

Butterflies return to Alston's stomach. The ceiling fan in the living room spins faster than he remembers. In the kitchen a radio plays music, big-band, the kind she likes. The bedroom has an empty bed with a flowered comforter. He creeps into the room armed with his line. She is not there. She could be out. He would wait.

Alston takes the butterscotch wrappers from his pockets and scatters them on the bed for ambiance. He takes off his black shoes. He undoes his belt and lets down his pants, stands in gold-lined white briefs. His untucked black shirt covers his pale upper thighs. It might make things easier nearly naked like this.

It occurs to Alston that Izzy might be in the bathroom, she uses the bathroom frequently. He steps out of the room and notices a faint streak of light from under the bathroom door. Alston can hear a rhythmic wheezing inside like a rusty rocking horse. Is the faucet dripping? He decides not to tap on the door. Exhaling, Alston enters the bathroom.

The gentleman caller is there by her side, pulling her close. He steps in small circles, pelvis and hip locked and rotating with the music. Rain on the roof cascades off the covered porch. The color of the houses and trees blur as Izzy turns and turns with the gentleman caller. His voice, even at her ear, seems distant and lovely. It finds a place in her chest and stays deep there.

I have traveled far to be with you, angel, he whispers.

Alston hasn't prepared himself for Izzy naked. He can see all of her flaccid imperfections tender in the water. He delivers his line, but she is slouching in the bath tub, leaning into the water, asleep and wheezing. She doesn't hear him. Water has spilled out onto the floor, his athletic socks are wet. The yellow tub with clawed feet looks like a beast devouring her. *This isn't right; she wouldn't leave the water dripping, why is she wheezing?*

The water is cold, Alston feels, she is cold as well. The wheezing sound makes her vulnerable, he lifts her head back carefully and her breathing comes deep and sonorous.

And I've wanted you, wanted this, Izzy says. They have found a rhythm now, dancing with the drizzle and the languid blues.

This is nice, he says. He tilts her chin, for what, for a kiss? Izzy lets her eyes flutter and close. Her hands stretch up the small of his back to his broad shoulders. Her fingernails against his shirt remind Izzy of clotheslines and bed sheets on Sunday mornings; soft fabric mingling with a lazy Southern breeze. His hair is moist with rain at the tips. Izzy's fingers tease it out.

Izzy, we've got to get you up, Alston says, forgetting his Southern accent. Wake up, now, what's wrong?

Alston shakes Izzy's shoulders gently. He reaches his hand behind her and works his way down her back to unplug the tub. Water drains loudly. Come on, now, we've got to warm you up.

Izzy doesn't weigh much, Alston thinks, as he lifts her from the tub. Her body doesn't have a beginning or an end, just soft pink flesh bunched together. This is different from the robust angles and sharp contours of women in the magazines. This is more natural, Alston thinks, maybe more human. It occurs to Alston that he hasn't been breathing through his mouth and his nose-whistle sings out like a warning. He quickly inhales and holds his breath.

Alston unsteadily steps forward. His socks slap against the bathroom tile and make footprints on the carpet in the hall. Big-band music from the kitchen punctuates his movement. Sax and bass and trumpet carry him into the bedroom.

Let's go inside, the gentleman caller says softly.

Of course, Izzy thinks, he would wait to kiss her in the house, properly. The rain has dissolved into a fine mist. Izzy hadn't noticed the absence of raindrops on the roof and the encroaching gray makes her feel uncomfortable.

Yes, she says, *let's go, let's go inside.* She smiles and bites lightly on her lip.

Izzy's feet are wet, the gentleman caller lifts her into his arms. They laugh together as he pushes past the screened door into the house, into her bedroom. The blues tiptoe down the hallway like an afterthought and linger in the corners of the room. He sets her delicately on the bed and undresses her, removes his own pants. Izzy lets a sigh mingle with the blues. His hands, despite their size, are light and patient.

Alston sets Izzy down on the bed. Her body clings to his soaked shirt as if she is unwilling to let go. She sinks into the bed, her head twists awkwardly on the pillow. Alston tries to right her neck. Her face is frigid. He pulls the flowered comforter down and covers her. Butterscotch wrappers flutter to the carpet.

Izzy has waited desperately for this, to be treated like she feels, like a woman succulent and alive. Her gentleman caller sprinkles rose petals on her and the bed, a southern romantic.

You're cold, let's get under the covers, the gentleman caller says.

It's true, yes, there is a draft it seems, Izzy thinks. His hands on her face are slightly cold. They could warm up together.

Alston glances at his body and is reminded that his pants are off. A lump rises from his stomach into his throat. She is too cold. The music from the kitchen has stopped for a commercial. Why isn't she waking? He puts his pants on quickly, the belt rattles as he struggles with it. His feet are cold in his wet socks. Things are turning serious, this whole idea was a disaster, he thinks, it could never work. The two of them are adrift and distant. Sex with Izzy? God, it never could have worked. Alston starts to feel for a pulse, but no, she's breathing, isn't she?

Izzy, wake up. Come on, wake up.

Shame and humiliation drive him out of the room in a panic.

The gentleman caller isn't responding to Izzy's body. Something is wrong, he is nervous. *What's the matter?* she asks, *it's fine if you want to take this slow, we're in no hurry, no hurry just now. We can talk, talk to me.*

He pulls his pants up quickly. Izzy doesn't understand. She watches his black-shirted back disappear from the room. She sits up and calls to him, *Don't go, don't go.*

Alston scrambles away from Izzy and into the bathroom because he might get sick. He is distracted by his face in the vanity mirror. The mask startles him. He takes it off and stuffs it in his pocket. A red mark circles his head where the mask had been. He washes his face with cold water. The mark remains, his nose-whistle returns. The faucet in the tub is still dripping. He twists it until his palm hurts. It still comes, the floor is a mess, his socks cannot get any wetter. A butterscotch wrapper has found its way behind the toilet somehow. There is a green towel hooked on the back of the door. He drops it to the tile.

From the kitchen Alston calls his father at the pharmacy.

Dad, he says, something's terribly wrong.

Alston, son, are you at a club?

Big-band returns unannounced.

Izzy's not waking up.

Louisiana?

Dad, I don't want to deliver to these people anymore, they are breaking me to pieces.

What are you doing there on a Friday? What's wrong with her? Don't do anything stupid. Is she still breathing? I'm going to call 911, let them handle this. I want you to go home now, son, I don't know what you're doing there, you're grounded. Do you understand me, mister?

Alston gently sets the phone in its receiver. He clicks the radio off and the kitchen falls silent, emphasizing his nose-whistle. The bag of grapefruit is still on the counter.

Back in the bedroom Izzy's neck is kinked on the pillow. The skin beneath her chin is stretched out and pale. Alston thinks of the tiny picture of the elephant in the newspaper article. The animal's trunk looked as soft and lifeless as her twisted neck.

Alston sits on the side of the bed and puts his shoes on. When he turns back to her, Izzy's face appears frightened, brows knitted, eyes glossy and blue. A strand of white hair sticks to her lip. Alston shifts his weight and delicately tucks the hair behind her ear. As if everything depends on it, he straightens her head.

That's better, isn't it Izzy?

He finds her wrist and feebly tries to locate her pulse. Nothing beats back from the thin blue veins. Alston closes her eyes and closes his own. His nose-whistle sings out loudly. It comes in quick bursts and looms over both of them like a stranger.

Adrift and Distant

Reginald Reed wakes up because his genitals itch. And the phone is ringing. And things were nice in his dreams. Kyla had come back.

On the phone is Minch Goriss, Head of Services. Reg resists scratching down there.

Reg, Minch says, I'm coming over, we need to talk.

Not something you can say on the phone?

No, obviously.

Why did you call?

Don't be wise. You're fired. You knew this was coming. But there's something else.

Reg swallows hard. There is a wasp flying near the buzzing air conditioner outside the window. What else?

I'll be there in fifteen.

The wasp is so blue it looks black. Kyla never liked bugs. Particularly the stinging type. She'd swat at them and whine in a high-pitched shrill. But that's South Florida. They met at the library. Reg had his hands to his head, pouring over a biology book. Sometimes he did this. As a Lawn Care specialist it is important to know the creatures in the grass. When to swerve around endangered species. There was a walking stick or something near a sand trap he almost clipped. So, to the library. He discovered it was a type of praying mantis. Reg took notes:

The Wondrous Praying Mantis: Who'll Answer Your Prayers?

The mantis waits motionless for an appropriately sized insect, camouflaged like a tree branch. At the right moment, this predaceous hunter of the order Mantidae, leans forward and snaps out with its front legs to capture its prey. It always starts eating the insect while it is still alive, striking straight for the neck to stop the struggling quickly. The male praying mantis cannot copulate while its head is attached to its body. The female initiates sex by ripping the male's head off...

Excuse me, we're closing.

Reg looked up and saw Kyla in a brown summer dress. She was petite and smooth-skinned with blemishless cheeks. She had a button that read, *Be a book worm.*

Oh, sorry.

There were palm marks on his forehead where his hands had been.

That's all right. Are you an Entomologist?

I'm not, but I wouldn't mind studying your beautiful eyes.

That's cute, she said, witty. I take it you're not an optometrist either.

No, Reg said.

You just like insects?

I mow the greens at the Boca West Community golf

course. I feel responsible when I hit something rare.

That's considerate.

I have other aspirations. There's plenty of time to think behind a mowing machine. I want to do something important, discover a new breed of butterfly. Maybe find where the unicorns have been hiding.

Kyla chewed on the outside of her lip. She was new at the library, down from Ocala, wouldn't mind dinner tomorrow at eight. Things worked out. She was healing from a recent relationship. Reg listened, understood, murmured affirmatives.

Time passed, they spent it together. At restaurants they enjoyed correcting spelling and grammar errors on menus. They discussed the classics, Reg ad-libbed. On off-time he read as many book jackets as he could. She was a Wordsworthian woman so Reg became a Wordsworthian man. Kyla couldn't stand the sight and smell of wet trash. Reg took great pains to walk closest to the street-curbs and distract Kyla when they approached anything like garbage on cloudy days. Reg wished all the waste would disappear from her life forever. Her black hair smelled like an exotic fruit. Reg learned that it was mango. She had incredibly desirable legs. No sex though. Then they talked about it.

It's complicated, she said.

I don't want to rush you, Reg replied.

She said he didn't understand and there were tears. Herpes. From the ex, Victor.

Oh.

Then Reg mentioned condoms.

Kyla's eyes wavered behind tears.

It's still a risk, she said.

Sure, but isn't love always? Let's take it!

They did, wonderfully.

Then Victor fell off a tractor in Ocala and lost a leg. Kyla explained that she had to go see him, he didn't have family, he needed support. Reg wanted to mention his own lack of family but figured this wasn't the time. She hung up and had since stayed away without word. Two months now. Last week Reg had the guts to send Victor a get-well card he hoped Kyla would see.

Minch bangs on the door. Fifteen minutes have passed, like that.

Minch is a hairy man with a hearing problem. He talks loudly. There is a tattoo on his forearm that looks like a swollen mess.

I thought I told you to pack up, Minch hollers.

Boca West Community is re-greening the golf course. No grass equals no Reg. Minch has explained this over and over. The makeshift apartment in the lawn garage where Reg has been living is being torn down at the end of the week. Also, when there is a lawn, it will be extremely fancy, Boca West will hire a team of professionals. Just Reg is not enough. Reg knows this, there was a memo. Minch suggested Reg look for work sculpting dirt with the Haitians. The Haitians have been hoeing and molding the earth in the heat since day one. It hasn't rained since Kyla left. Reg watched them working and was intimidated by all the sweat they shed hour by hour.

Soon, Reg shouts.

You speak with the Haitians?

I can't do what they do.

You've cut decent lawns, don't be intimidated by dirt. There's a place for you out there.

Thanks.

That's not why I'm here. There's been an opportunity. National Geographic Society is in town. They're researching toads. They say South Florida could be in big trouble. A photographer has been in touch with me. He's having trouble finding them en masse. Someone told him they hang around golf courses. You seen them?

You bet.

Reg had. Fat ones in the early morning hopping in thick St. Augustine grass. The talk among other Lawn Care Specialists was that toads were a pest and could be diced in the blade if they didn't jump fast enough. Still, Reg preferred to wait for a toad to move along.

Maybe you could get in touch with him. Keep in mind you represent Boca West Community still. Don't have hard feelings about us letting you go. Think seriously about re-texturing the earth with the Haitians. I could get you that job.

Sure, Reg says, distracted. He is thinking about toads and National Geographic. This could be a window. Things knock. Good work, hard work. He'd paid his dues in the field. He has tried to be animal-friendly. Sure, there was that squirrel accident, but the weed-whacker slipped. It could have happened to anyone.

Here's a card. His name is Doublait. Pronounced "Do blay." He's French. The number is on the back. I'm thinking Boca West could be mentioned in a caption. Everyone reads the captions. Go find lots of toads. I'd do it myself if I had time. And, if I couldn't find someone like you to squat behind bushes and gather the damn things. That's a joke, you ought to laugh.

Reg chuckles dryly.

Maybe I could pull some strings, land you something in the Painting Division. I know some steps that need lacquering.

I'll call him this afternoon.

Keep me informed. Get your stuff out of here. Demolition starts Friday. Can you swing a sledgehammer?

Reg gets on the horn to Randy Special. He is in charge of Special Lawn Care. He is fifteen and has a business cutting church-grass. Sometimes temple-grass. Randy owes Reg a favor after Reg called the principal and acted like his father. Randy had been skipping with a girl. Randy's father was in the Bahamas with a mid-life crisis.

Randy?

Yo, Reg.

Let me know if you see any toads, will you?

Toads?

You know, the fat ones, with the poison.

Why?

Just because.

You going to lick them?

No, that's ridiculous.

I've heard about kids getting buzzed on that shit.

You owe me.

Sure, sure.

At the library Reg doesn't see anyone he knows. They are probably not too thrilled with Kyla just up and going either.

The real name of the toad is Bufo Marinus. Bufo Marinus could be the ticket to something better, dignity and respect. Nobody questions National Geographic. From an amphibian/reptile book Reg takes notes:

Bufo Marinus: Beauty Beyond the Warts

Also known as the Giant Toad. Largest of the Florida frogs and toads. When this non-native species is threatened, it secretes a highly toxic milky substance from paratoid glands in the back of its head. Imported from Australia in the early 50's to help control rats and mice in the sugar cane fields. When eaten the poison can kill cats, small dogs, even infants.

Reg didn't know the dangers. Small dogs and cats were naturally curious. Every baby should be allowed to crawl in the grass. He checks the book out.

Reg hits the mall for a Polaroid. Then he hops on I-95 south. People on the road are in a hurry. Up ahead an askew sprinkler is watering the interstate median. There is a young man on a moped, driving uncertainly on the gravel, heading into the spray with a look of determination.

The amphibian park has nice lighting. Reg mentions this to the amphibian expert.

Really? the expert asks.

Nice overhead halogen hummers. Soft white and beautiful.

What are you looking for?

The amphibian expert is tall and tanned. She is wearing rubber gloves and a baggy scrub-shirt. Reg notes the tan-line from her bra-strap. Her mouth is just right, Reg thinks, she probably even eats soup gracefully.

Bufo Marinus.

This way.

There they are in their own room. The amphibian expert says her name is Brenda and she tosses her hair.

Reg starts snapping the Polaroid. Brenda asks what this is all about. Reg says maybe National Geographic. She applies pressure to a juicy toad's back so Reg can get the milky poison on film.

So, you're a photographer, Brenda asks.

Reg doesn't want to lie too much so he nods his head up and down and tries to look professional behind the camera.

They place a toad inside a blue baseball cap. They put one in water where it floats like a mulch chip. They silhouette a toad, profile it, sit it next to a frog.

While the pictures are developing Brenda explains mating habits. Reg says it'd be a good shot, the toads making love and all. Brenda suggests they dim the lights and they both enjoy a spontaneous laugh. Then Reg starts asking serious Bufo Marinus questions. He wants to know if South Florida should be worried.

She says, Heavens, no.

She could be from Canada, Reg thinks, the way she pronounces "Heavens."

Reg asks, What about cats, dogs, babies eating them?

That's rare. Most of the time the predator spits them out. It's a way to survive.

Brenda lets out a cry and points at two toads humping. There are wide smiles. Brenda casts a knowing glance which makes Reg blush. This could be the green light. Reg wonders if he should slip her his number.

You going to shoot them?

Reg looks at the smaller toad struggling atop the bigger female toad. He is having difficulty keeping balance. Still, he has a grin on his stupid toad-face.

No, I'll let them be.

Back home there is a letter from Ocala. It is from Victor. In it are traditional thank you things in polite cursive. At the bottom there is a messy P.S. written as if in a hurry:

P.S. I can't mention this to Kyla because she's very emotional right now, but there's something I've been meaning to get off my chest. Since I don't know you and you don't know me, I'm just going to put this out there. Kyla said you were a listener.

It was just another day in the field, sun was shining, a few crows were overhead…well, whatever, you get the picture, it was nice, the sky like it always is: above. I was thinking about a vacation, maybe Acapulco? Didn't see the stump. You run over the same ground for years and still miss things sometimes. Anyway, I was bucked off and pinned under the front tractor wheel. All the blood rushed up into my head as I helplessly lay there among the shorn stalks. When the blade took my leg I cannot describe the exquisite pleasure I first felt. I've tried to describe it. I've even tried to duplicate it. It's a kind of pleasure that comes unexpectedly, I think. Right before the wallop. I think the blood has to be up in your head first. I think you need to be seriously afraid—adrift and distant from yourself somehow. It made sense. Then I passed out from gushing.

P.P.S. Kyla is doing fine. She's sorting out her feelings. I should thank you for everything and hope you've stayed unaffected (sexually speaking).

Yours,

Victor

Reg reads this again. That last part is none of his business. Then he feels jealous. He knows he shouldn't, Victor is suffering, obviously, but he has Kyla. Would he sacrifice a leg to get her back? No, but still, he misses her. Reg wants to express this. He tries writing a letter to her: *Without you my heart has been like a wounded bird? Like a single pea in a pod? Like wind chimes with one chime?* These similes, Reg knows, are off.

On the phone Reg hears that Doublait doesn't have a French accent. Not when he says hello.

Hi, Reg Reed. I'm the guy you were trying to contact for the Bufo Marinus.

Terrific. Have you seen them?

Yes. I've got some shots maybe you could use.

Pictures?

I'm an amateur photographer.

En masse?

No, not yet.

I need to see dozens of them. The article has already been written. It's called "The Toads are Taking Over!" They are supposed to be teeming down here. Fat chance of that. I've done the best I can with the few toads provided. I was told cute yet disturbing. Elicit a sense of innocence turned rotten. Adorable little webbed feet; nasty, nasty warts. I nailed a beauty with a baby tottering over a pacifier next to a Bufo Marinus lurking in the weeds. People with feelings will eat it up. But that's not enough. I've got to see them en masse. My deadline passed last week. I've got dung bats to shoot in Indiana.

Maybe I could assist you.

Yeah, that's why I called your boss.

I mean, with the shoot. A photographer's assistant. I know we haven't met, but...

You're asking me for a job in photography?

I also do research. On short notice I found information on Bufo Marinus—also known as the Giant Toad. When this non-native species is threatened...

We have the facts. I need to see them en masse. That means a whole bunch of them together.

I know.

Is there any chance?

Isn't there always?

Actually, no. Your boss seemed to think you could find them. I can find someone else.

I'll do what I can do.

I'll be in touch with Mr. Goriss.

Reg sets the phone in its cradle. From a window he watches the Haitians. They wear broad straw hats and beige shorts, thin shirts. They keep low and rake the earth back and forth, texturing it. Clouds bunch up and rain falls. It's about time. The workers hold their palms out and lean against rake handles. The dirt will get heavy and wet and the workers will strain. Reg wonders if they mind or if the effort is worth the simple pleasure of awaited water on skin.

While packing Reg smells something funny. It is not his underarms. It is not in the closet. There isn't much in the closet except empty hangers. There is a rotting fern in the corner of the makeshift kitchen which Reg had been trying to sculpt into a bunny for Kyla. She likes Bugs Bunny much, the way the rabbit always tricks the others. Reg bought special scissors for the job but couldn't get the ears right. Now the plant sags. Reg has neglected to water it in several months. It smells like an old Christmas wreath. It is not the funny odor. Nor is the phone. Reg picks it up and dials Kyla's number. He has done this before, to hear her sweet voice on the machine. In the past his pride wouldn't let him leave a message, but now, after Victor's letter, maybe it is time.

The rain is pelting the air conditioner outside. The itch returns down there. The unanswered pulse on the other end is uncomfortable. Then Kyla's soft voice. It is hard to hear her; Reg presses the phone against his ear. She wants a name, telephone number, a brief message after the beep.

Hi, Kyla, it's me, Reg. Um, I was just calling because I got that letter from Victor. It sounds like he's doing better. In a way. That's great. Also, I wanted to tell you that I won't be living here for much longer. Minch needs the space. My phone will be disconnected soon and I don't know when I'll have the chance to talk to you again. Not that we're talking now, this is just me and the answering machine and maybe you listening sometime, but I don't know. That's just it, Kyla, I don't know. I don't know what happened to…

The machine cuts Reg off. The stench returns. Reg looks at his shoes. There isn't dog shit on them. There is pounding at his door.

Outside it is dark, pouring, and there is Randy with a golf club. He is wearing a drenched aqua shirt that says, "Special Lawn Care—I Cut the Straightest Lines!" Beneath this is a sketch of an awkward-looking lawn-mower zipping toward a phone number. The nine and five are about to be sliced.

Reg opens the door.

Whoa, man, we've found the mother load.

Randy is lanky with huge feet. He has blond hair and nearly-white eyebrows. His cheeks have been burned by the sun. The club is a rusty three-iron.

What are we talking about, Randy?

Toads. Hundreds of them. They've been popping up from the ground or something ever since it started raining. We're *golfing* them! You've got to try it, man.

No, I don't think so.

Why not?

There's no need to be cruel.

They're toads, Reg. Live a little.

I don't know.

Look, you asked me to find a bunch of these Bufo whatever's and I have. Now come on.

Randy turns and jogs off into the darkness. Reg hesitates and then has to hurry to keep up. The aqua shirt stands out. They weave between two mounds on the golf course that the Haitians have sculpted, around a canal, over a small bridge, and through a stand of pine trees to an unpaved cul-de-sac. The bones of a house are backlit by lightning. Reg cannot tell if the house is being built or if this is what's left after a fire.

In the mudded cul-de-sac are several kids; boys or girls, Reg can't make out gender, they are wearing slick orange and yellow rain-jackets. They clutch golf clubs.

See? Randy yells at Reg.

Reg watches a hooded kid race forward, square up, swing and connect with a hapless toad hunched to the ground. The sound is a not-unpleasant thud, like the flop of a softball against a bat. The toad soars in the air and drops near the house.

Yes, I see, Randy.

Want to give it a whack?

Why are you doing this?

It's fun, Reg.

Not for the toad I'll bet.

Didn't I tell you about kids licking them?

You mentioned it.

It'll make you high. In the wrong hands them toads are dangerous. We're protecting the innocent here.

I have read about baby accidents.

Precisely.

Reg figures he should call Doublait now.

Where are you going? Randy asks.

I'll be back. Randy, don't kill the toads. I know they're not perfect, but they don't deserve to be golfed.

Whatever. You need to lighten up some, my man.

Randy charges toward the others, targets a toad, swings, misses; swings, connects.

Back in the lawn garage, Reg calls Doublait. A machine answers and instructs Reg to leave a message. Reg says, Mr. Doublait, I've found what you are looking for. The toads are here. Give me a call.

Then Reg hangs up. Then he wonders if that was the right thing to say; *The toads are here*. The toads are not really here, they're under attack in the cul-de-sac. Soon, they may be dead or back in their hiding place. Reg thinks about calling Doublait and explaining. But, answering machines are starting to bother Reg. The message is never clear. Then he waits. For a while. Nobody is calling. Reg decides to take charge. He grabs a trash bag and returns to the cul-de-sac.

The kids are still golfing. The rain continues; thunder, lightning. The children aren't concerned about upraised golf clubs in the storm. Reg thinks maybe he should warn them. Then he sees some toads cringing next to the house. He snatches one. It secretes milky white poison and squirms out of his hands. Then he grabs it forcefully and drops it into the bag. He collects many toads. Then he struggles home with the bag. The toads jostle in his arms. He will put them someplace safe and wait for Doublait to come over in the morning to shoot them. Reg looks for someplace safe in the lawn garage. Nothing occurs to him. Then he goes to the bathroom. There is weed poison under the sink, but that's it. He removes the poison and unloads the toads there. He closes the doors. The toads scuttle around. Then Reg wonders if this many toads equals en masse. He has doubts.

Reg returns to the cul-de-sac, where the children are still golfing. He cups his hands to his mouth and yells, Watch out for the lightning. One kid pauses mid-swing. The others notice and pause themselves. They all face Reg and let their golf clubs hang to the ground. Reg thinks he has reached them. But they don't move. After a while, Reg feels uncomfortable. He quickly gathers a bagfull of toads. When he looks back at the children they have advanced a few feet toward him. He hurries home and locks his door. He adds the toads to the others under the sink and decides this is enough.

While washing up in the sink, the stench returns. It is not his hands. It couldn't be the toads, they smell more like formaldehyde. When he takes his shoes off Reg discovers a crumpled and green lizard inside his right shoe. The tail is missing. Reg wonders if he picked it up at the amphibian park. Maybe he should contact Brenda. He hopes it isn't endangered. It is rank, regardless. Reg flips through the amphibian/reptile book. The best Reg can tell, from the lizard's condition, it is a Carolina Chameleon. He notes:

> *Hiding in your skin: The Carolina Chameleon.*
>
> The Carolina species in the family of color-changing lizards is distinguished from other chameleon cousins by its extraordinarily long snout. Native to North Carolina, this reptile can be found from as far south as the Everglades all the way north to Pennsylvania.
>
> When crushed and carried in your shoe all afternoon, the Carolina Chameleon smells remarkably like the bitter scent of wet and rotting garbage on street-curbs. If you whiff this, be careful. It is a warning. Things sour without explanation. Next time make sure your shoes are empty or go without them completely.

Reg wakes up because his genitals itch. And the phone is ringing. It could be Kyla. She might be coming back.

Reg squishes a toad when he steps out of bed barefoot. They have escaped. The toad rolls over and plays dead. Reg thinks it is play. He didn't put all his weight into it. Reg hurries into the kitchen.

On the phone Minch screams like he always does. It is all Reg can do to resist scratching below.

Reg, I've spoken to Doublait. He called this morning and told me you could have been more courteous on the phone with him yesterday.

What did I say?

You wanted his job or something. But that's not the point. Focus on toads.

I've found some. They're here.

Are they photogenic?

Reg pauses.

That's a joke again. You need to work on social skills, Reg. You're not a bad worker, not that you're the best, I've seen you slack-off on the hedges.

Which ones?

By the pool. The lifeguard agreed. You're too timid with the lawn equipment. Just get in there and chop. You're not making art.

How would you feel if you decapitated a squirrel?

I thought you were over that. Didn't I give you the afternoon off?

I guess I needed more time.

You've got it. Remember, you're fired. But that's not the point. You need to be more amiable. That's only one of the points, actually. The more important one is that we're coming over. To see the toads. Be there in fifteen.

There is white poison on the underside of Reg's foot. He hangs the phone up and wipes the stuff off. Then the urge is too much. He glances down his pants. There are blisters nestled in his pubic hair. He scratches himself unmercifully. In the makeshift bedroom Reg sees the toad he stepped on is still playing dead. Then the phone rings.

What? Reg shouts into the receiver.

There is a long pause.

Reg?

Kyla?

I got your message.

You're in town.

No, I've been checking my machine from Ocala.

Oh. How have you been?

Fine.

I think about you all the time.

Reg, I'm staying with Victor. He needs me. I think I need him too.

Reg sits on the floor. He massages his chin.

Thanks for informing me.

This is all new to me, I can't explain. I'm sorry.

God, Kyla.

Please don't make this harder than it has to be.

Reg shakes his head. I guess I should have seen this coming. You never even loved me did you?

Reg.

After everything I did. I tried to read poetry, I wore that cologne you like, I opened a savings account, I took up sculpting, I sent Victor a get-well card...

I'm going.

We had something nice.

I think you were a rebound.

Great. You gave me herpes.

There is silence on the other end. Reg listens to Kyla breathing. Then he hears the line click. Then the recorded operator tells him that if he'd like to make a call, please hang up and try again. If you need help please hang up and try again. A toad peeks at him from under the refrigerator.

By the time Minch and Doublait arrive, Reg has only located three toads, including the dead one he stepped on. The others could be anywhere.

That's not en masse, Doublait says.

What do you think of these pictures?

Minch and Doublait regard the Polaroid shots of the toads from the amphibian park.

Blurry, out of focus, too light. Is that your thumb? Doublait asks.

There's a frog in here. I told you toads, Minch says.

I wanted to compare and contrast.

Oh, la, la, I didn't come here to see pictures. You're not getting my job. National Geographic doesn't use this crap. All I wanted you to do is find toads en masse, Doublait says. You're wasting my time.

There is a place, Reg says.

Minch and Doublait look skeptical.

Reg sets out across the golf course. The Haitians scatter between the mounds. Reg leads Minch and Doublait down the canal, over the bridge, through the trees to the cul-de-sac where Randy and his friends had golfed the toads last night. Reg notes that the house is being built, it is new, the framework is bright and strong in the daylight.

What the hell is going on? Minch asks, out of breath.

Toads, Reg says, down there. He points.

The men peer at the toad carcasses in the mud.

A bunch of them.

But they're dead, Doublait states.

Does it matter? Reg asks.

Of course it matters, Minch says. Are you an imbecile?

People won't notice in the photograph. I'll set them up around that house in animated positions.

Reg begins to pick up dead toads. Several have intestines in their mouths. They are slimy and Reg drops a couple as he arranges them in front of the house. Maimed Bufo Marinus are everywhere. The children had a field day last night. Minch is trying to whisper to Doublait about how Reg has lost his mind. He points a finger to his head and twirls it saying, Cuckoo, cuckoo. Doublait has his hand to his chin where he massages a small patch of hair.

Don't you see the symbolism? Reg shouts, wiping his hands on his pants. This new house represents progress. Human development. The toads will look as if they stand in the way. It's ominous. People will shiver and worry. They'll believe. Don't shoot any close-ups.

Minch is outraged. His face colors.

Doublait finishes rubbing his chin and sets a camera on a tripod. We'll give it a try, he says.

Minch quiets.

Reg sets the least damaged toads up front and the most mangled ones in the back under shadows.

Through the lens Doublait mentions that the shot may work after all. He shoots and shoots. For a couple at the end of the roll Reg underhand tosses a toad into the frame to capture movement. Birds swoop low and Minch chases them away excitedly. The house poses patiently as the sun dips through clouds above.

Doublait is genuinely impressed. He pats Reg on the shoulder and says that though the idea was grotesque, it was creative. He recommends Reg look into working at the dump. Waste Management could use that kind of energy.

All the same, Minch says as the three walk into the stand of trees and back toward the golf course, it'd be best if we kept this afternoon under our hats.

Doublait agrees.

Reg feels nauseous. Then he hears commotion back by the lawn garage. He jogs forward with a hand on his stomach. Minch and Doublait follow.

The Haitians have stopped working and are standing around the two mounds of earth holding their tools defensively. Randy has an idling push-mower in his hands. He has chased the elephant two blocks from the Methodist Church on Glades Road to here. Police sirens are encroaching. Then Reg sees the animal kneeling in water between the mounds.

The elephant has been shot in the head, on the shoulder, the stomach, and several times on the back. Someone has clearly blown away a tusk. Reg approaches it. Randy shouts over the running lawnmower that this is a bad idea. The elephant lets out a cry and shakes its left hind foot. Everybody takes a few steps back. People shout as Reg advances. Police have arrived. Minch doesn't know what to do. Doublait readies his camera. The elephant has huge black eyes. They are calm despite the excitement, as if the elephant were elsewhere.

Reg reaches out to massage the elephant's trunk. It whips away. A police officer demands Reg step back.

How can I help you? Reg whispers.

The elephant drools. The spittle is mostly blood. It heaves forward, attempting to stand. Reg has no time to jump out of the way, but it cannot rise. The left hind foot juts out again as the elephant sinks back to its knees. The police are ready to fire, they don't see an alternative, they aim away from Reg and wait for an opportunity.

Your foot, huh? Reg asks. He hurries around to the back of the elephant. Police hesitate. Doublait's shutter snaps and clicks. Minch has decided to play with his hair. The Haitians are still on guard with rakes and hoes. Randy's lawnmower runs out of gas and sputters off. Water splashes. There's metal embedded in the elephant's heel. A railroad spike. Reg stretches forward and grabs it, yanks.

Then the elephant kicks backwards. After two

shakes the spike comes out. Reg is thrown hard to the ground. The elephant falls onto its side with a loud popping sound. It is as if pulling the spike out punctured the animal. The pop is gunshot. The police unload their bullets. A stray cuts through the elephant's ear and clips Reg in the arm. He drops the spike. Blood rushes to his head. He glances over at the elephant. Its eyes are pinched shut in folds of wrinkled skin.

Reg wakes up because his genitals itch. There is some sort of cream down there. He is shirtless with a circular bruise on his chest, over his heart. A nurse enters the room and explains. He is in a hospital. He kept scratching in his sleep, doctors applied the cream. His arm is healing in a sling, the bullet wasn't deep. The bruise is from the elephant's foot. Somebody is here to see you.

Who? Reg asks.

A woman.

Kyla?

Brenda.

The amphibian expert?

The nurse shrugs. Should I let her in?

How long have I been under?

Off and on, two days.

Oh. How do I look?

Honestly, honey, you look beaten.

I thought so. Let her in.

Brenda enters the room with a newspaper. She is wearing a skirt and a flowered shirt. Reg watches her mouth as she speaks.

I thought I'd come see how you were doing.

How did you find me?

The paper. There's a nice shot of you.

The entire front page is dedicated to the elephant incident, with the exception of a short write-up on a kissing bandit. Apparently, the elephant was roped down and ready to perform tricks at the Margate Swap Shop when it stepped on one of the stakes holding the binding and panicked. It trampled a woman and her baby, damaged cars in the parking lot. In the back of the paper is a shot of Reg holding onto the elephant's foot being thrashed. The caption reads: *Local Lawn Care Specialist Reginald Reed inexplicably attempts to wrestle the elephant to the ground.* The article mentions that he is recovering from minor injuries at the Boca hospital.

You're not a photographer.

Reg shakes his head, no.

There are reporters outside waiting to hear your story.

What?

People want to know why you grabbed the elephant.

There was a railroad spike in its foot.

That was brave.

What can I say about the mother and baby?

Nothing, of course. Does this hurt?

Brenda tentatively sets her fingers on Reg's bruised chest. Reg flinches. Then he reconsiders. He sucks his breath in and puffs his chest out as big as he can. The pain in his heart is enormous but for now her hand is enough.

Shirtless Others

A thin woman waits to slice the Mako shark with a butcher knife. This is the last shark of the competition and the biggest my lover and I have seen. This one could be a winner.

Come on, my lover says to me, *it's almost over*.

Her cheekbones are pink in the salty air. I had just told her that I didn't like this. I said it as if I didn't mean it. We've been inside the air-conditioned condo all weekend. Somehow being outside has made me claustrophobic.

The shark's stomach looks like a silver-lined moon glistening there in the stale afternoon heat. The crowd has gathered in a semi-circle around the butcher. Five fishing gentlemen leer at their catch from a rocking boat. They make me seasick bobbing so close to land.

They win. Their Mako carries the most weight. The fishermen thunder. The crowd is all smiles and cheers. My lover lets out a holler and raises her arms, arms that have fingers with nails that left deep and passionate stripes down my back. I've had to wear a shirt in a crowd of shirtless others.

The thin woman cuts into the neck of the Mako to bleed it. She slices the shark's soft underside. She digs into the belly. Several baby sharks spill out onto the pier and gasp. They writhe in the air with unblinking black eyes. My lover doesn't see this, she is moving with the crowd to congratulate the fishermen. Those watching are quiet.

I wait to see what the thin woman will do. I am prepared to cry out if she skewers them, protest, maybe point a finger. But she lets them be, dying like they are, on the dock.

Some Storm

My sister is pregnant and I am on the hill fighting to find
her a suitable husband. Our father is absent. He went to
work, said maybe he'd visit mother for a spell. Mom's
losing her memory in a retirement community. My father hobbled out of the house with his mahogany cane,
slammed the screen door early this morning. Then May-
Renee told me she was pregnant. We were in the kitchen.
There is no father, she said. She wanted to say more. She
was still in her bathrobe; I noted that her ankles were
pink and round. I was cooking corned beef hash and
eggs. Toast toasting in the toaster jumped just after she
told me. I didn't ask questions. I took her to the cellar
and hand-cuffed her to the hot water-heater. She pro-
tested, mentioned our father over and over again. I told
her he had nothing to do with nothing. She had better
hope I straighten things out before he got back.

It's like my sister to blame our father. He is an old
man with yellowed teeth and a decided stench. He has a
gut like a fisherman, sallow eyes; he is overbearing and
simple because he is still alive and he is still the father.
He is easy to criticize and my sister takes great pleasure

in doing so. She blames him for keeping the lights in his room on after midnight and complains that he keeps her up with his struggling up and down the hall clicking his cane against the hardwood floor. And when he drinks, she nags. These things do not bother me, I sleep downstairs. I put the handcuff key in my overall pocket and said to leave Dad alone. She mentioned I didn't know anything—I don't see things clearly. I told her I'll know enough soon and left her down in the cellar—a good place to think things through.

I posted a sign in our neighborhood that read, *If you've even thought about rutting with my sister, meet me on the hill, someone's responsible*, and then I signed it. The hill is in our backyard. Everyone in town knows about the hill. It is a place where things are decided. I figured men who wanted her would come and challenge me. I figured whoever knocks me off the hill makes a good husband. I may not actually find the bastard who stuck it to her, but at least I'll find someone who could handle me. I'm wiry, a cougar, I surprise with my strength.

I didn't figure there would be so many people waiting to fight me when I returned from posting the signs everywhere. Such a crowd who'd thought about doing it with my sis. I know most of them—some fathers already, a dog-catcher, a few haggard boys, alcoholics, Uncle Tim. They form a crooked line and look more like a rag-tag parade than manageable suitors. There's not a man among them I'd be willing to embrace as in-law.

When I'm in place I spit on my hands and lean low. I hear mumbling anticipation roll up the mount and pass over me. I say, Let's get it, then.

First one up the hill is Brett Updyke, a slob who works at the slaughterhouse. He's got a short stick which he carries like a dagger and tries to thrust it into my eyes. His shoulders are like Texas. We grapple, I keep low, chat.

I'd make a good father, Davey. We never really done it, but I make an honest living, Brett says, taking hold of me.

You kill hogs, there's blood under your fingernails, I say. I don't trust you know how to keep her happy. She reads.

I surprise him by tickling his ribs. His arms slacken from my shoulder and I shove him, with my foot behind his legs, backward down the hill. I kick at the dirt and clap my hands, crack my neck; try to establish a fighting rhythm.

The next man up is Bobby Stetson. He used to date May-Renee back when we were in high school, she still in middle school. I remember hearing him describe my sister's thighs to a group of boys in shop class. He mentioned that they, her thighs, were like dinosaur crap. I hit him a few times right there in class, but the teacher broke us up. It's true, she has a little extra down there, but it's nothing that ought to get outside the family.

Bobby's got a grin and something behind his back.

I just came here to claim what I've already done known. Knock you up, too, nutcase. When I'm finished, I'll go fetch my prize, get me a son.

This taunting doesn't bother me, language can be cruel, and men just talk to men this way. Bobby brings a fence post from behind his back and smacks me in the neck with it. I am choking, but otherwise all right. Bobby is still grinning and I notice he is missing a tooth, third from center, bottom row. I don't remember when he lost it. He punches me in the mouth and I stumble back but keep my feet. Although Bobby has higher ground, he isn't bright. He tries to kick me in the nose. This doesn't work, I grab his leg and spin him around, catch him in the chest with my elbow, he exhales and tumbles down without his grin.

My cousin Dexter, Uncle Tim's son, wants to give me a try. We don't call him Dexter; he can't stand the name, so we call him Tripod because he was born with three balls in his sac.

Davey, Tripod says when he's up with me, I don't mean any disrespect on your sister, but the truth is I've had her in my head a time or two. My Pappy thought it best I come up and have it out with you.

I can appreciate that, I tell him, he'll make a decent husband maybe someday.

He tries to bite me on the cheek, cut me with neglected fingernails. I get scratched, poked in the eye. I can't help knowing what I know and it is easy enough to kick him squarely in the scrotum. He's got more pain than most men down there and topples off the hill.

In the crowd my Uncle Tim is twittering, embarrassed by his son. I want to tell him I'm sorry for all this, really. I shout down to him that I'm obliged by family support. He nods up at me, tries to salute, I think, or maybe the sun is heavy in his eyes. The day is in motion.

I built a fence for the man who is now ascending the hill to meet me. His name is Ivo. I build fences for a living. I remember building this man's fence because I noticed that his lawn, the lawn I was building the fence around, was festooned with condoms. Condoms on the trees, on a small bench, stuck to a hibachi, and, I figured, shortly after I finished, probably on the fence. I asked him about the mess and he told me that kids liked to sneak into his yard at night and behave like animals. At the time I found his wording a bit curious and I told him so.

I mean they really grind against each other like a pitbull on your leg, or cows against barbed wire, he told me.

It was true about cows and fences. I've seen clumps of fur dangling from the wire I used to fence them in. Sometimes they just rub themselves raw.

I asked Ivo if the fence I was building was to keep the kids away and he shook his head. He told me that he had heard that neighbors had been spying on the affair, an affair that happened all the time although mostly in the moist morning hours between two and four, and that the fence was to keep things discreet. He didn't want the neighbors watching. I didn't ask any other questions.

Ivo, now, coming up the hill, has a cardboard box under his arm. He is an older son of a bitch, glasses, probably pretty smart; the kind of man polite women might call a gentleman.

How about you and I playing a board game up on this hill?

I don't know what he is talking about. Board games don't make sense, they don't prove anything. The idea here is brute strength. The best man is supposed to dethrone me for my sister's hand. That's not confusing.

I don't think so, I say.

Well, why not? Ivo asks.

What's the game?

Ouija.

That's nutty. I'm the only spirit up here.

Tiddly Winks?

I remember those. It's been years. I suppose we have time for a quick game.

He sits cross-legged on the hill and withdraws two plastic cups, one yellow, one blue, and an array of multi-colored plastic winks. I kneel down beside him and take a handful of pieces. He stretches forward and places the cups, one in front of him, one in front of me. I'm blue.

I am at a loss of words so I ask him about the fence.

It's fine, he says, just fine.

I do not want to ask him about my sister. I do not want to ask him about my sister at all. I do not want to know if my sister has been in his backyard, maybe with Bobby Stetson grinning, grinding like cows grind against barbed wire.

You know, he starts, your sister's sly, I've got to hand it to her. I've seen her creep out of the shadows and snatch the condom-sacks immediately after the boys toss them. Peculiar, I thought at first, but then I saw what she was doing and it makes sense now. I don't think she likes men. I think she really wants a baby, though.

This, I don't want to hear. I concentrate on putting the plastic winks in the blue plastic cup in front of me. I am losing. I don't know what it means if he wins. The hill is not for Tiddly Winks and thinking. I shouldn't have agreed to play. I ask him why we're doing this.

I don't know, he says, I just enjoy playing.

I imagine him in his empty house at two or three in the morning with his Tiddly Winks, probably not play-ing as well as he is now, and I feel sick. I grab him by the shirt-front and lift him to his feet, his glasses slide down his nose. He is not heavy and rolls gracefully down the hill.

I'm not sure what Ivo was talking about. Maybe he

mistook her. It was dark, I'm sure. What would my sister want with used condoms? It's ridiculous. Ivo's mistaken. My father and I do our best. With mother gone it's been up to Dad and I to explain what it means to be a good young woman. I ordered glossy magazines and Dad makes sure he's there should she need him in the night. We never talked sex though. I didn't at least. I figured she knew it was a bad idea. And now look what happened.

She's been staying out late lately, I've noticed. And she's been visiting our mother too frequently. She stays at the retirement community a long time, long enough for me to maybe be suspicious. She could be using Mom as a smokescreen while she ruts with someone. One of the ancient puds at the home still firing crackers? No, the few times I've visited nothing caught my eye. Something could have happened while Dad and I were at work. I've been busy building a ten-footer around the cemetery. Seems children have been painting the headstones bright colors and stealing flowers. On lunch breaks I always came home to visit May-Renee. I never noticed anything fishy. Come to think of it, though, the mailman walked with a lilt last Saturday that I thought was unnecessary. Was he wearing cologne? I haven't seen him in the crowd today. The bastard couldn't even adjust his route and show up here like a man.

There is a woman, long blond hair, firm breasts, tall, I've seen her around, a friend of May-Renee's; coming up the hill to meet me. She's carrying a turtle. Vulgar men hoot down below not knowing what else to do.

What's with the turtle? I ask when she is on top with me.

Look at it. The woman holds the turtle out toward me with the underside exposed. I can't see anything.

Look closer. The turtle is squirming, its tiny head making tiny circles. I lean closer and notice that someone has carved the initials M.R.B. and J.A.G. with a heart in between, into the shell's soft underside. My sister's initials are M.R.B. I suppose this is J.A.G.

That's nice, I say.

His name is London. We're taking May-Renee away from here. You are a pig. You can't treat women this way.

You're talking about my sister, I say, I've known her all her life. Maybe when she marries she can be crazy. I'm trying to help here.

You don't understand her like I do. She's unhappy.

Everybody is, of course. But we're a family. While my father's gone it's up to me to get to the bottom of this. I don't even know why you're up here. I can't hit you.

The crowd below is antsy. They are bored with all this talk, I'm sure. The sun has peaked and is heading on. I wonder what May-Renee is thinking about down in the cellar, cuffed to the hot water heater, still in her bath robe. I should have let her put some shoes on.

I'm up here because I'm in love, O.K. London and I are taking her from this.

Look, I say, you didn't get my sister pregnant. You wouldn't make a good father. I am sure of this. The turtle is endearing, but otherwise useless.

Where is she? J.A.G. screeches.

In the cellar, I say, and feel something hit the back of my head. The crowd is throwing rocks. A knot begins to rise. I am hit again, this time on the arm. J.A.G. lets out a quick cry, clutching the turtle to her chest. A rock smacks her in the jaw. She tries to give me a fierce glare as she backs timidly down the hill. I tell her where she can find shoes for May-Renee and to comfort her as best she can; I'm going to figure it all out soon. Oh yeah, and despite what you think I love her too, that should be obvious. I'm not exactly enjoying this you know. J.A.G. spits almost nothing in my direction.

I drop into a crouch and cover my head with my arms. A man cradling a bottle of whiskey is staggering up the hill. Rocks have missed him thus far, but he seems like an easy target. When he gets to the top he tries to focus his eyes on me. I tell the drunken bastard to look out. His hair is mussed up, frazzled, dark and swaying above his head. I don't think he knows why he is here. No way could he have read the sign in this condition. He moves forward and collapses because he is drunk and that's all there is to do.

Soon, the rocks stop. Some storm blows in without warning to wet things down and then passes without much energy. People leave, disappointed. Fine by me. Let them think what they want. I'm still up here, aren't I? I don't know who the father is, my sister doesn't have a husband, but our family is intact. I've done what I can do. If Dad were here he'd be proud. The community has been tempered, everyone has had a shot, and all they can do now is gossip.

I eye the bottle of whiskey still in the drunk's hand. I could use a gulp. The knot in my head is throbbing. Nobody's coming up the hill—it wouldn't hurt to have a nip. As I'm lipping the bottle I hear a noise I cannot describe—like sheet-metal in a thunderstorm, like the whir of a bottle on a tabletop, like the sound of my father as he struggles up the stairs in the evening, only amplified. It is hypnotic.

Under a willow tree I see an ancient man bending

a long saw back and forth. He looks like he escaped the retirement home and crawled here on his knees. The saw is shiny and new. He probably stole it from some distracted carpenter. On occasion he taps the blade with a short metal rod to keep the sound moving. Everything is vibrating in my head. With effort I stand. This man is a great distraction. I don't know what he is doing, don't know what the sound is supposed to mean. Is it some courting gesture? No, it is not pleasant like that. The man is too old to have sex anyway; it is all he can do to hold himself upright and play. It's more like some mythic dirge.

Lost in that noise, things just go dark and then turn reddish—like night happening and then, poof; sunrise. Someone has sucker punched me. I drop and am rolling down the hill, listening to the saw, glimpsing, as I roll, my father shaking his cane where I once stood, saying something; or maybe the souse has arisen and wants his whiskey back. I do not know—I cannot see clearly.

Whoever is atop the hill is telling me how I am a fool, how I do not understand what it means to be a husband or father, how I'm a drinking neophyte. I suppose these things are true, but I do not care just now. I don't need the criticism. For a moment I'm not even worrying about my sister. I'm just hearing the saw make noise like rain rushing through an old gutter, like a train grinding against the rail, like the wheezing of my father as he struggles down the stairs to greet me in the morning.

Mother May I

May-Renee hears her father clicking his cane and wheezing down the cellar stairs as he comes on, looking for atonement. The father, like the others, had thought about having sex with May-Renee. Her bathrobe is open more than she feels comfortable with but there is nothing she can do hand-cuffed as she is to the hot water-heater. A woman named Jefery keeps May-Renee company in the semi-darkness. May-Renee mentioned that her father had wanted to hump her and it was a shame. Jefery set a turtle with the initials M.R.B. and J.A.G. carved into the underside, a heart between them, on the cool ground. May-Renee is M.R.B. and Jefery is J.A.G. The turtle is a token of Jefery's love. It, the turtle, named London, disappears into the shadows, forgotten, upstaged by all this.

May-Renee wants her off-white bathrobe closed. She's been in the cellar all day, thinking. When the father gets to the bottom of the stairs Jefery screeches and charges him. There is pent up anger. A draft teases May-Renee's breasts and makes them itch. Her feet are bare and cold, nobody brought her shoes, her exposed ankles are pink and round. Davey, her brother, tried to find her a suitable husband up on the hill after she told him she was pregnant. Jefery slaps at the father's face and kicks at his old legs. The father steps back and tries to square off using his cane for balance. It's nice that her brother cares, May-Renee feels, but he is too concerned with right and wrong to understand the situation. There is no need for a husband. She told him that she was pregnant but didn't exactly know who the father was. Jefery screams that the father is a dirty bastard. The father wants to know what the hell is going on, who is this harpy, why have things come to this. There is no need for sex, really, it hurts; May-Renee tried it once with a high-school boyfriend and bled. The boy had recoiled in shock. Jefery has a little drool on her chin. The father is pushed back up the stairs with a flurry of windmill punches, claws and all. The two stumble outside. May-Renee fertilized herself through a series of messy encounters at Ivo's house. She bites at her bathrobe collar and manages to cover part of herself. She wants a girl, a baby girl with pretty brunette girl-hair. She's aware that there are too many men in her life. London, in the corner, makes small noises as he scuttles against the wall. He sounds like the handle of a *Racer Flyer* wagon dragging backwards down a concrete slope.

Over dinner that evening, after Davey uncuffs May-Renee and massages the places she had been chafed, everyone eats pork. Jefery makes it. The father sits with his head hunched and his silverware clutched in his fists. Occasionally he leans in to maw some meat. Davey eats slowly and winces because the back of his head, where he was blindsided by his father's cane, hurts. There is swelling. May-Renee eats everything Jefery places in front of her. There are snap peas and gravy-biscuits. She loosely listens to their conversation:

I'm going to stay here and watch things over, maybe cook sometimes because May-Renee shouldn't be struggling around food. I'm keeping my eye on you, Jefery says.

I didn't *do* anything, harpy, the father replies. She looks like her mother back when.

Why don't you visit your wife more?

Look, it brings me down.

I want what's best for her, Davey says. Clearly, there's a puzzle piece missing. We need to plug in a father, a husband, maybe a decent man. The three of us are limited.

Wrong, Jefery says. Wrong. I can be your everything enough, Plum.

Look, May-Renee, I'm sorry about all this, the father says as he massages his dry hands. I didn't do anything. If you'd feel better about it I'll go see a priest.

What about Mom? Davey asks.

Son, watch yourself.

Why'd you hit me?

In order to get up sometimes you've got to fall down. Don't go acting like you know something when you clearly don't or I'll smack you again. That's love. Toughen up. Make me proud.

This is about May-Renee, Jefery shouts. Take this father/son crap outside.

Everyone turns to May-Renee who is mopping up her plate. There are crumbs on her collar. She blinks deliberately. After dinner she finds her way to the bed upstairs and sleeps. Things grow from the inside.

Good-morning, Sleepy-Winkie, Jefery says to May-Renee

as she comes down the stairs from rest a few months later.

Morning to you.

Jefery has cut her blonde hair short and spiked it with gel. She has given up on earrings, toe-rings, finger-rings; everyring. She has a surprise turtle tattoo on her inside thigh, new and green. Jefery is holding tightly to a memory of May-Renee. They've kissed once, awkwardly under a sycamore, without tongue, nothing inappropriate, just a passing girlish thrill for May-Renee. But Jefery fell unmistakably. She has a few years on May-Renee, just turned twenty-two, and is old enough to be confident in her homosexuality. There have been instances of masculine misbehavior in her past, nothing she wanted to get into, really, just bad *things* young men tried to do. That was past. Now Jefery cannot control the stirring in her chest when she watches May-Renee in motion, any kind of motion.

You must be hungry, Jefery says.

Yes, do you know how to make pancakes?

Since the kiss, Jefery initiated several strategic touches; a caress on the arm, a soft-playful pat on the ass, a quick sweep through the brown bangs framing May-Renee's face. She stole a peek down May-Renee's blouse while she slept, in the third month. She couldn't help but blow softly until the broad nipples stood tall under the thin rose nightgown. Shortly after came the turtle tattoo.

May I?

Sure, yeah.

Jefery places her hands on May-Renee's stomach. She circles the belly-button with her palms. She lifts the yellow shirt with shaky fingers, eyes on May-Renee's eyes. Slowly she bends down to kiss the soft pink skin. She kisses again and again, cooing and breathing.

How about some pancakes? May-Renee says awkwardly, pushing Jefery's head away.

Jefery stops kissing and stands. Have you felt kicking?

I think that's what woke me up. I'm going to make pancakes.

No, no, I'll make them. You sit.

I don't want to sit. Where are the men?

Working, as usual.

How have they been behaving?

Adequately. Your father has been sulking. I let him look in on you twice and both times he twittered and shook nervously. I told him to seek psychological help. He hasn't been to see your mother since you went to bed. He mentioned the worms don't like grape.

The father owns two acres of flat land where he farms worms. The secret behind his success, which is impressive in the worm-farming industry, is to sprinkle the topsoil with Pixie Stick sugar powder. The worms eat it up.

Davey?

For a while he kept trying to find out how you got pregnant, Jefery says. He conducted interviews and nosed around the YMCA. He requested a different mailman for some reason.

Did I get any mail?

Not that I know of. Are you expecting something?

I ordered *Today's Mother*.

Do you mind me asking how it happened—who he was?

Yes. Pancakes are burning.

Sorry.

When the pancakes come, she sits at the table. Butter and syrup. The first cakes are burnt, but Jefery cooks on; they improve. May-Renee eats everything placed before her. She grows fatter in the belly, inside kicks, she lets Jefery feel, Jefery is tickled, giggles, the spatula in her non-feeling hand drips batter. They both smile.

She's going to be beautiful, Jefery says.

Yes, yes she is. Mother will be proud.

I love you.

There is a pause. May-Renee stops chewing. Then Jefery wrings a dishtowel.

I don't know how to respond to that, May-Renee says. She pushes her chair from the table, reconsiders, slides forward and eats more pancakes.

Batter drips. Jefery moves to the sink, sets the spatula down, gets a towel, bends to clean the mess. That's O.K., she says, softly.

May-Renee doesn't fully hear this. She asks, What?

Nothing.

No, you said something.

I have a surprise for you. Jefery stands and lifts her skirt to expose the turtle on her thigh.

Is that a leaf?

No, it's a turtle. It hasn't healed entirely.

I'll bet it hurt.

If you kissed it you'd make me feel better.

May-Renee is silent, fork and knife in hand, eyes on the table. There is syrup on her chin. Jefery points it out, tries to dab it with a napkin.

I can get it, thanks, May-Renee says, fending off Jefery's hand.

Will you ever?

May-Renee had been licking her lips, but she quickly pulls her tongue inside her mouth. No, I don't think so.

The stove burns off whatever was left in the pan. A thin trail of smoke rises.

Look, you are like my sister, May-Renee says. I want you to be an aunt when the baby comes. The stove is still on.

Jefery has a shattered look on her face, like an over-cooked statuette in a kiln. She is thinking about turtles; London fenced in chicken-wire out back, the bruised tattoo on her thigh. Turtles were supposed to be special, they represented endurance, patience, resistance. Jefery wrote a pocm that compared love between women as soft and delicate like the body of London and unity between lovers as impenetrable as his shell. It took time for love and unity to blossom, but once flowered, it lasted for a hundred years or more. Just like a turtle. Jefery is still working on end rhymes and trying to untangle the metaphors, but the idea is there.

May-Renee stands, turns the stove off, takes the pan and places it on a cold burner. Thank you for breakfast, she says, and for staying here and helping out. You don't have to stick around, you know.

Oh, Jefery says, I don't mind. Let me know if you need anything else. Ever. I'll get it, I don't mind. You don't have to tell me you love me back, that's not why I told you, I understand you've got a lot of things on your mind.

May-Renee steps out of the house, the screen door slams shut.

On her way to the retirement home May-Renee stops at the *Party Palace* for two balloons. The exchange inside:

Hey, May-Renee, haven't seen you in a while, you're starting to show, do you know what it is yet?

A baby.

Ha! No, no, sex.

The gender? It's going to be a girl. How did you know I was pregnant?

Well, your brother has been nosing around. Oh, and your stomach is bigger than I remember.

I want a yellow one and a pink one.

The clerk, who has one gray eye, one green eye, is wearing an apron with a pouch, has mild arthritis though he shouldn't at his age, has been seriously tempted to turn vegetarian, and has had, on numerous occasions, unsavory thoughts about specific party favors in aisle six; he fills the pink and yellow balloons with helium. The rubber skin stretches, first pink, then yellow. Strings are attached. Money transacts. Niceties are exchanged and May-Renee is back in the car, on the road, the balloons like passengers kissing roughly in the back seat. They rub together and make rubbing sounds.

The old guard at the gate smiles at May-Renee as she slows the car and waits. He comments that he hasn't seen her in a while, Laura-Leigh is hanging in there, just as spry as a butterfly. Congratulations on being pregnant. The gate opens.

May-Renee says, Thank you.

Laura-Leigh, the mother, lives with two elderly female roommates who are not memory-challenged. They are happy to see May-Renee. Laura-Leigh is happy in general. The balloons catch sunlight and cast shadows over the tightly-made beds. An orderly grins with extremely thin lips and says to Laura-Leigh, See the balloons?

With strings in her left hand and her mother's hand

in her right hand, May-Renee leads Laura-Leigh out to
a picnic table in the middle of a small field behind the
community. Wind pushes the balloons backward; May-
Renee's stomach carries them forward. At the picnic table, they sit on benches across from one another. There
is a strand of gray hair draped across Laura-Leigh's smiling mouth, it sticks to her teeth.

Let me get that, Mother.

Laura-Leigh looks at May-Renee, at the balloons, at
the sky, near the sun, and down at her blouse which fits
uncomfortably, one breast gone, one breast sagging and
dry, back to May-Renee; smile intact.

I've missed you.

The mother cradles her head in her hands, her smile
bunches up. May-Renee can see the gap in the middle of
her mouth where she lost a tooth. She mumbles something, her tongue makes small curls between her lips.

May-Renee attaches the balloons to the picnic bench
and pulls two index cards and pens from her pockets.
She places one pen in her mother's hand and directs it to
an index card.

Say something wild, Mother, write something naugh-
ty if you'd like, May-Renee says. Write about when you
were younger and all the men hounded you. When you
were fine and careless. Remember that picture of you
with a cigarette? You were so hot and confident, Mom.

May-Renee begins to write on her index card. When
they finish, May-Renee will tie the cards to the balloons
and let the balloons free. She has been doing this with
her mother for nearly a year now, more frequently in
the beginning. May-Renee thought it would be an ex-
cellent way to communicate with her mother, maybe
understand how she felt inside. At first, it had worked,

Laura-Leigh had written, *I Want To Remember How To Cook!* on a card and was reluctant to release the balloon, May-Renee had to yank the string from her fist. Then they held each other and rocked and cried softly. I will try to help you remember, I will try to help you remember, May-Renee had said and repeated. The second and third times they released balloons, Laura-Leigh's messages lacked clarity. She had written, *Momma wants a birdie*, after May-Renee explained that the balloons went up in the air, and, *Give it back*, when May-Renee mentioned that somebody out there would likely find the index card and read the message. The notes tapered off in lucidity as the mother forgot and forgot and forgot. One time, however, May-Renee read, *I want a baby*, on the index card. They had talked about it, sort of, the mother twirled a strand of hair as May-Renee asked what she meant by a baby.

You want a child? May-Renee had asked.

The mother clucked her tongue. Her eyes seemed sharper than usual, to May-Renee.

You can't have one, you know that.

The mother was silent. Eyes moved skyward. They released the balloons and Laura-Leigh stared at the ground.

Since that incident May-Renee had been thinking about children herself. If she was going to have a baby it had better be before Laura-Leigh passed on. She wondered if it was enough to just want a pretty girl. She decided to ask the sky. On an index card she had written:

I am a woman who wants a baby.

1257 Willow Court

Baton Rouge, Louisiana 70802

That yellow balloon had gotten caught on a lamp-post before it ever left the city. It deflated and drifted to the ground in a rainstorm. Jefery had been on a jog when she found it and visited. The two of them talked adoption. This was out of the question as far as May-Renee was concerned, the agency would never allow a child into a house like the one she lived in. Her father's proclivity for drinking and spitting and remembering the old times would never pass any adoption test. Besides, May-Renee was sure that she was too young, and it was important for the child to come out of her body. This frustrated Jefery, but love requires flexibility. Jefery emphasized that May-Renee wouldn't need a husband. She said, Men inevitably make decisions with their genitalia and that is wrong, wrong, wrong. This logic made sense to May-Renee, her brother and father often behaved without thinking things through. Davey once took a boyfriend of May-Renee's atop a hill in their backyard for a rumble after Bobby had said something rude about her thighs. The name-calling didn't bother May-Renee. Bobby was a stupid boy who still had a night-light and masturbated in the morning curled in a whimpering ball. May-Renee witnessed this after tutoring him in Algebra for hours and falling asleep on a couch. When she went to retrieve a pencil in his bedroom, there he was. What bothered May-Renee were the direct actions after her brother sauntered down the hill victorious, the way Davey's nose bled all over his shirt. Such cocky bravado. Yes, she had said to Jefery, I see your point.

So, May-Renee came up with her plan on getting pregnant. She told nobody but her mother, who forgot or else never comprehended, and the index cards. While her mother wrote: *Cheese, cheesse, chese*, May-Renee wrote about Ivo's backyard. The first card said; *I've decided to have a baby (preferably a pretty girl) and I want to have it before my mother completely loses her mind.* This blue balloon went into the sky and floated to Florida where an old man who still golfed despite his bad knees found it wrapped in his television-satellite, read it, scowled, threw it at his garbage can, missed, bent to pick it up, cracked his back, stood up and emphatically shoved it into the trash while rubbing his spine. Another card read; *Tonight, I stole into Ivo's backyard where I had heard that people of all ages (though mostly high-schoolers) come to have sex. I watched couple after couple sweat and groan in the heat and nothing about this act excited me.* This green balloon pushed into the sky and over the ocean where it bravely drifted as far as it could before exhausting itself in the water. It was eyed by sea-turtles but never eaten; it sank into the muck. A card read; *Forgive me, Mother, I know you would not approve, but I've decided that I'm going to take the discarded condoms that these boy/men toss around the yard and try to squeeze the sperm out of them into me. I've been using your turkey baster.* This red balloon didn't make it out of the field, it had a leak and limply bounced along ten feet from the earth. May-Renee watched it sputter out of the field and catch in a tree in the block of *Sunblest* suburb next to the retirement community. She feared someone would discover it and pass judgment. When she tried to fetch the balloon with a long stick, a bulldog barked and barked at her until she reluctantly drove away. A fourteen-year-old girl saw the balloon and waited half a school year for it to come down. When she read the card she was disappointed.

Well, I've done it, I'm pregnant Mother, you're going to be a Grandmother, May-Renee says, today.

Laura-Leigh is slowly drawing a square on the index

card.

May-Renee writes; *I'm going to be a mother. Everything worked out. Thank you, God.*

Let's let these suckers fly, shall we Mother?

When May-Renee pulls the index card from Laura-Leigh's hand, the pen makes a line from the center of the square down off the paper. The balloons rise and wink out of eyesight, first yellow and then pink.

Back at home Jefery and the father are fist-fighting in the backyard. Davey is slouching in a lawn chair sipping whiskey and watching. He has an index card in his lap. When May-Renee approaches, he straightens up.

You're getting bigger.

Thanks. How long have they been at it?

Beats me. I just got home and there they were. Jefery seems especially angry today. Oh, by the way, you got this index card in the mail and I think I know what's going on.

The index card reads: *I'm tired of everyone treating me like a sex object. I'm my own person. My baby will be her own person too; we'll be our own people together.* May-Renee had sent the card via a black balloon. She hadn't addressed it and doesn't know how it found her.

I've read it about six times and I still don't think it makes any sense. The mailman brought it. He found it in the cemetery and assumed it was you, based on the hand-writing and your looks and all. So he said. Truth is, you've been bopping that skinny mailman haven't you?

No, dummy.

Well, he's off our route. I eighty-sixed that son-of-a-bitch. Have you ever really looked at him? He's got nose-hair almost down to his lip. It's like a moustache.

I don't even know who you're talking about.

Fine, fine, suit yourself. What's done is done. I think it will be good to have a little one around here. There's a lot we could teach it. By the way, that's a fine friend you have there. She's got a solid jab. Keeps Dad honest.

The father and Jefery keep swinging at each other landing soft punches mostly.

The baby boy is born in a thunderstorm. The father, Jefery, and Davey do their best to keep May-Renee covered as they rush her from the car to the emergency room. There aren't any complications. Around town, lightning struck the high-school football field goal. The *Baton Rouge Gazette* mentioned the birth in the Locals section. It read:

While the storm whipped Baton Rouge yesterday local May-Renee Blandford gave birth to a healthy bouncing baby boy. Though the father of the child wasn't in attendance, May-Renee's own father, a girlfriend, and her brother were. Concerning the absent father, Davey Blandford said, "There's no need for another man in our house. This boy's going to have his hands full enough with us."

On behalf of the Gazette, I'd like to welcome Baby Blandford (May-Renee did not reveal the child's name) into our community.

The thunderstorm subsided by the time everyone returned to the house. An old office was set up for a nursery. Jefery had insisted they paint it pink, certain the infant would be female. May-Renee said that it didn't matter, there would be plenty of time to repaint things. The child was sleeping with her for now anyway. She retired to her room for two months. The family tried to think of what May-Renee and the child might need and put it outside her door. Everyone tensed when they heard the boy cry. Talking about the baby as the "boy" or the "child" became frustrating. They wanted to know what to call the child officially. Davey thought the kid should be called Max—a simple, tough name. Jefery suggested London. The father thought, maybe, Junior. They climbed the hill and fought about it. Tensions soared.

When May-Renee came out she told them to call her boy Lee, after her mother.

On her way to the retirement home May-Renee stops at the *Party Palace* for three balloons. The exchange inside:

Oh, he's adorable, coochie-coochie-coo! Ain't that something special?

Thanks. I'd like a yellow one, a pink one, and a blue one.

Sure, yeah. The clerk fills the balloons with helium: Blue, yellow, pink. He can see May-Renee doesn't want to talk. She rocks the baby in her arms forcefully. Strings are attached. Money transacts. Niceties are exchanged and May-Renee is back in the car, on the road, the balloons like passengers kissing roughly in the back seat, Lee in the front with his eyes everywhere.

The old guard at the gate ohhs and ahhs. Eventually, he lets May-Renee through.

Laura-Leigh is happy when she sees her daughter and her grandson. She had been happy before she saw her daughter and grandson, May-Renee knows. She places the baby in Laura-Leigh's arms though the orderlies think it is a bad idea. She thanks them for their concern, puts one hand on her mother's back, holds the three balloons in her other hand and walks out into the field. The wind pushes the balloons backward and the baby in Laura-Leigh's arms leads them forward. At the picnic bench the mother and May-Renee sit across from each other. The baby is placed on the table. He cries. May-Renee ties off the balloons, withdraws three index cards and pens, guides her mother's shaking hand to the card where she starts to scribble, and then picks up the baby.

Lee continues crying. There is nobody else around. May-Renee lifts her shirt and directs his mouth to her right nipple. The boy suckles. Laura-Leigh stops scribbling and stares at her daughter. May-Renee's right breast has gotten lumpy recently. She thinks it is because her glands are filled with milk. One particular lump is cancer. Laura-Leigh smiles at her daughter and May-Renee smiles back.

Yeah, I know, it's a boy. That's fine; he'll be a good boy. What are you writing today?

Laura-Leigh's eye twitches and doesn't stop.

Write something wild, Mother, write about your grandson, how handsome and bright he's going to be.

Laura-Leigh leans heavily on her pen.

I know, I know, it's going to be hard at home. I won't let him be like them. He will be like you or me, only male.

Laura-Leigh starts to write on the card again. Lee sucks greedily making sucking sounds.

That's it, Mom, write about how Lee is going to grow up and be the best man in the world. He'll never forget you. He'll remember the wild things, those wonderful years. I'll show him pictures. I'll buy a camera. I'm so glad you are here with him now. It's very important that he knows you. That you know him.

Laura-Leigh draws a circle on her card. She traces it over and over again.

OK, Mom, that's something. May-Renee pulls Lee from her chest and places a pen in his tiny hand. She covers herself. The boy cries, but quiets as May-Renee forces him to mark his card with an X.

X's and O's, that's the two of you, kisses and hugs. Lee = kisses and Mom = hugs. I'm going to write that on my card. Now, may I please have your card Mother?

Laura-Leigh continues to draw circles, roughly. The pen bruises her soft hand.

It's all right, Mother. Let me have it. These three balloons are special. They're going to travel way on up to the moon or the sun or God.

Laura-Leigh tentatively releases her pen and slides the card across the table. May-Renee sets Lee on the ground in a patch of dandelions. While she attaches the cards to the balloons Laura-Leigh plays with her fingers. She looks at May-Renee, up into the sky, at the picnic table, into her lap, at her feet, and at the curious child preoccupied by the weeds.

Slight

When I'd do sit-ups J.D. put all her weight on my feet and leaned over my knees, insisted I keep trying. She had these gray eyes I wish she could've seen somehow without having to rely on reflection or a picture; they saw things maybe you didn't want her to see. This was physical education on the island of thick grass inside the track. We all had red and white gym clothes, red shorts. I'd grunt and lift, my elbows like horns jutting from behind my head, again and again. When I got tired my knees spread apart and I'd lift myself mostly with arms and neck. J.D. never held my legs together too tightly. She'd keep her hands on my kneecaps and stretch her body forward, getting serious, *You can do this, a few more, come on, come on.* I'd keep straining, rocking, motion like sex, or, more honestly, like labor, she the mid-wife demanding something born from me.

I believe in ghosts and am frightened by them though I'd never admit it aloud. We can rationalize: That shadow in the courtyard is a father, that high window has a neighbor just looking out like you; *You see it's gone.* There's nothing uncommon about a woman cutting her hair in an empty room, shutters clattering outside, eyes sharp to the glass, searching for a little change.

J.D. and I took walks through the forest after high school. She'd spot a snake every time and point it out to me. I'd go after the dull-colored ones, catching them sometimes by the tails, or behind the neck, or I'd miss them completely and stumble. We ducked spider webs and followed familiar trees until the distant traffic mumbled away. Sitting Indian-style, finally, in a small clearing, she'd lay out cards and tell my future. There was a freckle under her left eye separate from the ones on her cheeks. Her collarbone made a little space between neck and arm when she stretched forward to uncover a card. Her hair fell around her shoulders nearly purple in the filtered sunlight. I let my mind imagine touching her because I knew I wouldn't act. J.D. was in a place I didn't understand, my hands were awkward. When she knew my thoughts were on her, knew maybe because my life was as simple as the cards in the dirt, she'd sharply glance up and catch me with a smile. I'd retreat from her eyes, find the isolated freckle and try to control the color rushing to my face. *You are a really caring and sensitive man with a good talent, one of the most important, the ability to love*, my cards said, she said.

J.D. walked into a hardware store somewhere in California the day before Christmas and asked for a length of rope.

The attendant behind the counter asked, *Is this rope for hanging?*

Yes, said J.D., *you know that.*

Sure, the man said, *I'll find something that will do.*

When J.D. did her sit-ups I sat on her feet and reclined against her legs. I watched the rest of us struggling. J.D. kept mostly quiet as she rocked behind me. The only sound I remember is a soft thud as her slight spine beat down the crabgrass. If something wrong was being born within her, I didn't know. I was on the other side of the country tucked into a warm bed, comfortable that Christmas was in the morning, packages beneath the tree, fragile ornaments dangling half-noticed somewhere deep in the branches.

Leaving

My grandfather moved into our house with his old age and brittle legs when the leaves were good and ready to fall. The house could accommodate this. My parents transformed the foyer, which was for our muddy shoes and wet coats, into his bedroom. We used a side door as the entrance and exit. It needed a firm shoulder to open. I was man enough to handle it but my sister struggled. My grandfather let her use the front door and pass through his room. The kitchen started to collect clods of dirt from my sneakers. I kicked them under the refrigerator.

Polly and I were told by our mother that he had fallen into a deep funk and needed attending with his bad legs and all. That's what she told us. I overheard her tell him that he was there to watch us kids after school, be our babysitter since she was returning to work. She works at Bordt's Potato Chip Factory, *Bordt-A-Rooney-Roo!* On a windy day our neighborhood smells like chips. Mom comes home reeking of Sour Cream and Onions or Barbecue. I didn't like the idea of being watched by the old man—I was fourteen, I could take care of myself and Polly. Our father didn't say anything about this new affair, he kept himself busy at his cigar shop downtown. When Dad comes home, late lately, he reeks of cigars. My father doesn't smoke himself, he just likes the smell of others' smoking. Sometimes he'd bring a fat one home for my grandfather to smoke slowly. I tried a Tiparillo once, secretly. It burned my eyes.

I decided to keep an eye on my grandfather and Polly because they started spending too much time together. She's my only sibling and I think she needs my guidance. She almost drowned in a puddle when she was a baby. I had been pushing her stroller along and let it soar down a hill around the block, *Go Speed Racer*. It tipped and she plopped into muddy water that had been collecting from unseasonable rain, deeper than I thought it should be. My parents squawked, retrieved her, fed me soap. They sent me to Sunday school, gave me braces, and pre-mature acne. I still have plenty of zits; they linger like caterpillar cocoons on leaves.

Polly is starting to look more like our mother. She has defined cheekbones. There's a little scar on her forehead from the stroller accident that I've learned not to notice. She doesn't giggle anymore; I heard her laughing like an adult, playing pick-up-sticks with my grandfather. When he laughs it sounds like something in his chest is breaking up. I peeked in on them playing sticks in the living room and there they were just playing and laughing. His legs were folded normally, I thought.

My grandfather's name is Hodge and so is mine. I thought this was neat for a while, *Hey, Hodge, you sure are a great guy!* I could say the same thing and he wanted me to. I realize the old fuddy is just trying to get by, I don't know exactly why I've decided to dislike him. Instinct, survival of the fittest, the town's only big enough for one

Hodge. I've thought of changing my name.

The old man is too thin and his eyes are often runny like over-easy eggs. You never see him without his loafers. He's quiet in them. The other day he tried to teach me how to play my drums, in the basement; poof, he appeared. He heard me in a fine snare-roll and came down to talk about it. He said, More wrist, more wrist. Hold the drumsticks like this. He demonstrated with the sticks between his wrinkled thumb and forefinger. He kept crashing the cymbal with this loose-lipped grin. I told him it was great. He said, Now you try. I slipped into an uneasy tom-tom rattle. He folded his arms behind his back and unloaded old-man advice: It's good that you're releasing pent up aggression via some instrument. I used to play the tuba, you should try out for the high school marching band next year, it could make a difference. Then he changed gears, just like that, said he was someday going to be gone and it was important for him to give us grandkids something to remember him by. I skipped a beat and he noticed. I stopped playing and tried to give him my undivided attention. We were quiet for a while. Then he tried to talk God with me. I kept my back straight and nodded. Even God wanted someone to preach the faith, thus Jesus. He wanted me to agree with this. He wet his lips in anticipation and scratched his wrist until white flakes of his skin fluttered out into the filtered light from the storm shutters. I blinked. Polly bounded down and asked, Whatcha doing? I stomped the pedal for a heavy bass boom and said, Nothing, nothing, nothing.

My best friend Jed (actually Jed Jr., but nobody wants to be a Jr.) and I play the Leaf Game. We've waited three seasons for this. Above us are oaks. Jed and I stand in the yard and catch falling leaves. The driveways are off-limits; they are deep pits that drop down into the center of the universe full of fire, or they are moats within which are spikes and crocodiles, or they are full of mines, or quicksand, tarry goo. If you step out there you lose automatically. Jed likes to lean over the driveway to snag a leaf, but I stay clear and work the middle. The idea is to catch the most leaves. When he catches one he calls out a number and crumples the leaf. When I catch one, I don't say anything and shove it in my pocket. That way he never knows how many leaves I've caught until we're ready to quit. I keep a mental tally and if I've been losing, I'll sneak a couple leaves from the ground while Jed's being a hero at the edge of the driveway. It isn't easy to catch a falling leaf, they hang in the sky forever sometimes. You never know where it will finally land, the wind carries each one differently. I don't have the knack Jed's got, I know, but I win sometimes in my own way.

Old Hodge and Polly are in the backyard on the trampoline. It takes up most of our lawn. My father overdid it. He brought it home in pieces that wouldn't quit. Once it had been assembled the whole family jumped up and down for a few days. I mean the whole family at once. It wasn't any fun jumping alone. I tried. I climbed to the middle of the navy-blue stretched canvas, shoeless, of course, and made a few timid hops. I got into it. I tried a flip, landed on my ass, sprang up onto my feet. I kicked my legs out but not too far out, old enough to be protective of my groin. I was cautious but it didn't matter, after a few minutes I felt I couldn't stop. There was only navy-blue tarp and a blurry universe. My hands flapped ridiculously. I tucked my legs and tried to slow down on my knees, which knocked me to my stomach and eventually bounced me a few times on my face. My cheeks stuck to my braces. I felt a cherry growing on my forehead, but at least I was at rest. Breathing heavily, I crawled on my belly across the trampoline and rolled off. Nobody used the trampoline for a while and it started to sag. Grass grew beneath it. Now my grandfather and sister have decided to give it a try. Old Hodge is on his back and Polly is hopping next to him. This way he doesn't have to jump and can still experience the fun of bouncing. They're both having a good time. I wander out back and shove my hands in my pockets. I hum something western and kick at the earth. I find a rake and make a pile of leaves. My grandfather looks as if he's going to lose his teeth laughing so damned hard. Polly's already grown adult teeth. I tell a joke but nobody's listening. I make the pile as big as I can. I say, Watch this, but I'm not fooling anyone. I run and jump and get poked under the eye by a stick. I am too old to cry so I get up and kick the hell out of the pile.

Autumn develops. There aren't as many leaves to catch anymore, and the odor of fall, which we smell only when downwind of Bordt's Potato Chip factory, has a bite to it.

The tops of the trees are skeletal. My grandfather and Polly have been lingering around me the past few days. He whispers to her when he thinks I'm not looking and she points at me behind my back. I'm pretty sure they're judging me based on some quirky young/old understanding of things. He and I attempted to play a friendly game of Connect-Four yesterday after dinner but it didn't work out. He kept blocking me from placing my pieces in a row and never once tried to win himself.

Polly observed us from the green couch. We played five games, I was always red, he was always black. I'd get three in a row and he'd block me. He'd get three in a row, have the opportunity to win the game, and then put the checker-chip in an irrational spot. I thought about cheating, distract him by reaching over and swatting his leg, say I thought I saw a fly; sneak an extra piece into the slot to seal my victory. The problem was, Polly would see this, I knew, she'd tell our grandfather. Finally, I said, Just beat me old man, quit toying.

He said, This isn't toying, I'm not trying to win, at my age that's no fun, I just want you to not win too. Polly and I are waiting to see how you treat your family when you get frustrated.

I looked at Polly on the couch. She smiled.

Why?

We want to see if you are like your father. A cheater.

I didn't know what the old man meant.

Did you notice he was late for dinner again tonight?

I had, actually, didn't think anything of it. I just wanted the game to end. We played again and nobody won, or, I guess more correctly, we both lost. I went to the basement and made racket on the drums. When I hurried by the old man I purposefully bumped into his legs and didn't excuse myself.

Thank God for the Leaf Game. Lately, I've been taking risks and standing near the driveway. I've been crumpling the leaves like Jed. I don't know what's come over me, I've just grown tired of playing it safe. High in the branches is a brown nest where squirrels live. It looks like a coon-skin cap for the Green Giant. I point it out to Jed. He says, No way, it wouldn't fit the Green

Giant's head. I argue, which he doesn't expect from me. The Green Giant is not super-huge like King Kong or anything. Besides, it just looks small because it's way up there. Jed says, Duh. We don't speak for a while.

Fifteen, I shout, and crumple the leaf loudly. He's on twelve.

When I look toward the house, the blinds in the downstairs window close quickly. My grandfather is spying on us from his room. I imagine my sister is with him. I've given up on being a good brother, the old man has won her over. That's fine. I'll just catch leaves.

What's with your sister? Jed asks.

Of course he would ask this. Jed doesn't have braces or zits. Polly has always had a crush on him and hasn't been showing it lately.

Thirteen, he says. She keeps staring at me.

That's my grandfather.

No, fourteen, upstairs, don't look now, in her bedroom window, fifteen. Damn, it almost hit pavement. Did you see that?

I look and curtains swish upstairs.

Where are you going? Jed asks.

I'm going to check this out. Parents are at work. The side door tries to hold me back. The kitchen is messy. I pass the foyer/grandfather room on my way up the stairs. He's quiet in there. I don't knock on my sister's door.

What's your problem?

Polly isn't startled. She's sitting slightly turned toward the door, in front of the window. She can see everything this way. A gerbil named Fatso, in an aquarium, opens sleepy eyes. Fatso never runs in circles around the spinning toys. Every time I see that little creature I have to grin a bit, even now when I'm trying to be stern. In front of Polly is a sketchpad and crayons, she's sitting on a green-plastic chair.

Why are you spying on us? I take a few steps into the room and look down at her sketchpad. She covers it. I try to take it from her. She doesn't cry out and doesn't let go. Finally, I get it. She's been trying to draw us playing the Leaf Game. Jed has an orange oblong head and a purple smile. There are red leaves as big as airplanes in the swirling yellow sky. I'm a tan stick figure with a brown mouth like a zipper, arms out-stretched rakes. It seems I'm stuffed with a little straw. The driveways have sharks in them, not a bad touch. She kicks me in the shin, says, Give it back. I am prepared to in just a minute when we both hear our grandfather clearing his throat in the doorway. Those damned stealthy loafers.

Hodge, what are you doing?

I could say the same thing.

He's wearing an off-white turtleneck that seems to dip in the chest as if he's missing something there. In his hand is a notepad with a pen tucked into the spirals. I tell him nothing. I'm taking this confrontation personally and will hang onto the sketchpad forever now. They can gang up on me all they want, I'm not letting go. I'll show the picture to Jed, we'll laugh out loud, Ha. It's good, the picture, I wouldn't have made the leaves so big, but Polly is moved by my having it and that makes all the difference.

Hodge, son, my grandfather says, you know we've been watching you.

Sure, I know this, so?

I'm teaching Polly how to learn through observation.

No, you're just teaching her how to spy.

Polly folds her arms and reclines in the plastic chair. She's staying out of this now.

My grandfather smiles and steps into the room. His legs look fine. The smell of potato chips have penetrated Polly's room, *Bordt-A-Rooney-Roo!*

We don't think we're spying.

Polly doesn't nod to affirm the old man but doesn't not nod either.

I hug the sketchpad to my chest. You're spying, you're spying, I say. I take a step backward, closer to the window. With the curtains closed, it's tough to see outside. I wonder if Jed has gone home. My grandfather takes a solid step forward.

I think you really get to know a person by watching them without their approval. You see what kind of character they have.

He's setting me up for one of his old-man lectures. He had his chance to say something interesting when he first got here, he blew it, now I'm not listening. Somehow I think he's gotten thinner, the turtleneck makes him look like a skinny turtle. I don't know how genetics work, but I pray to God that I don't turn into him.

I'm not giving the pad back, I say.

Does this surprise you, Polly? he asks.

She shakes her head, no.

You see, she's not surprised that you want to hurt her.

Don't try to turn her against me, Satan!

Hodge, son, that's a little harsh. Not surprising, but harsh.

I know about Satan, I've done Sunday school.

You read the whole Bible?

Well, no. I've read the Satan parts. All I know is that

you've been an evil influence on Polly. Before you came she was cute and naïve. Now she's drawing pictures that make me look like a scarecrow. She never would have done that before. I'm no great brother, I know, but she could sketch me better. Did you see the zipper mouth she gave me? It's brown. What's that supposed to mean? Everything I say is crappy? Before you came she would have given me pink or yellow lips.

All I want is for you to be fair and return Polly's pad. And maybe read the Bible more thoroughly.

No. I hug the pad tighter and crease a corner.

Fine, my grandfather says, but remember that we've been watching for a while, learning about you. We know you cheat at the Leaf Game. You pick leaves up when Jed's not looking, don't you?

Of course, damn. You can't play the Leaf Game by yourself, he knows this. If you catch a leaf and nobody's there to notice it's like you didn't catch one at all. Jed will feel betrayed and find another friend. My grandfather's trying to cast me out of Eden, instead of an apple he's using a leaf. Well, sort of, I'm the one who cheated, but still.

What, are you going to tell him? He won't believe you.

He'll believe us.

I follow his eyes to Polly. She's not smiling but she doesn't look unhappy. My grandfather holds out his hand. His fingers are wrinkled beyond repair. I toss the sketchpad at Polly. She doesn't catch it. I go to my room, lock the door, and throw a tantrum into my pillow.

Fuck it, I think, and jump on the trampoline, alone. I know this isn't brave, the tarp is sagging, but what else can I do? I keep my shoes on and feel less naked. I'm sure they're watching. Fine by me, maybe I'll moon them. Potato chips hang heavy in the air, the sky is almost edible. I try a flip and don't do badly.

Note it.

Jed appears and slings an arm over the side of the trampoline, takes everything in. He has a way of being perfect. I know I'm not man enough to tell him I've been cheating, just come out with it and burn my grandfather.

There are still leaves falling, wind's picking up, Jed says.

I stop jumping gracefully. Fine.

Out front leaves fall. The wind picks up. Jed is exceptional today, deft. My heart's not in it. I'm thinking about shoving him onto the driveway. I haven't always been hostile, last spring I gave an old woman my umbrella because it looked like rain. Then it poured and I sneezed for a week. Mom and Dad were proud. Now I'm going to ambush my best friend? Jed's never done anything wrong. His father, on weekends, takes him to the Ground Round. They invited me a few times. You're allowed to throw peanut shells on the floor there. My father works on weekends or goes out of town for exotic cigars.

My sister and grandfather inside might be surprised if I knocked Jed down. It's tempting. I'd show them a side of me they haven't seen, *I'm mean, Watch out!*

Jed's got his eyes in the sky. I hear him catch his breath. A small squirrel falls. Jed leans out as if. The thud on the driveway is real. I imagine that the squirrel family up in the nest has their paws together hopefully, peeking through the branches. The squirrel isn't moving, except for the tail, which rustles in the breeze. Jed and I are at a loss on the grass. There's a half-crumpled leaf in his hand.

The front door opens and Old Hodge steps out with my sister. Polly has her sketchpad and a red crayon. They walk down the driveway and stand over the squirrel.

Interesting, my grandfather says.

Interesting, yeah, Polly mentions, bad luck three.

How so?

I saw this squirrel jump across the driveway, from that branch to that branch twice before he tried it just now.

Huh, bad luck three, yeah.

Jed steps onto the driveway and joins them over the squirrel. He asks what we should do.

Old Hodge crouches down to inspect. Polly stands close in case he needs to steady himself on her. This is ridiculous, there isn't anything wrong with his legs. That was a lie from the beginning.

He asked what should we do? Polly says.

Yes, dear, I heard him, Old Hodge replies. We're going to have to put it out of its misery.

Hey, I say, Jed and I should decide, this is our game.

They ignore me.

Hmm, says Polly.

Jed folds his arms.

From where I'm standing I don't see any blood.

How? Polly asks.

Get a big rock from the garden, I suppose. End the suffering.

Jed says he doesn't need to see this, he's sorry about the squirrel, he's going home, he runs off down the street. He's the fastest runner around, he'll be there before he knows it.

Polly chooses a rock the size of her head. She carries it with both hands to our grandfather. A leaf falls to the grass next to me.

Don't do it, Polly, I'm going to tell Mom and Dad.

Your mother would agree with us. Even if your Dad happened to be around and actually listened to you, tattletale, your mother would rebuke him. He's in the doghouse. He's been cheating himself, Old Hodge says and coughs. This is the first time I've heard him sound unhealthy, there could be phlegm in his lungs. I had forgotten that he will die soon because he is old. At the moment, though, I can't have sympathy.

What the hell are you talking about? I ask.

It's true, Hodge, we've been watching, my sister says.

Our father?

He's been cheating on Mom and won't admit it. I asked him and he changed the subject.

I swear the squirrel is twitching. Old Hodge holds the stone carelessly.

Maybe he hasn't been, ever think of that?

We've got evidence, Polly says. His clothes smell like lavender and they didn't used to.

Perhaps it was a customer at the shop.

We think that's where he first met her, but they've been secretly meeting at hotels. I found a book of matches from the Comfort Inn in the garbage can.

Why were you going through the trash?

It was my turn to take it out. I just happened upon them.

Maybe he needed them to light customers' cigars.

You know he has his lighter.

It could have been out of fuel.

There has been lipstick on his collar.

Could have been Moms.

Mom wears *Crimson Moon*, this was more, *Scarlet Sunrise*.

Dad wouldn't do it, Polly.

Check out his posture, his gait, his guilty eyes; I've got notes. He told me my spirit reminds him of someone sweet he knows.

That's just Dad, he's a little corny, it has nothing to do with smashing a squirrel with a rock. By the way, since when do you go around using words like 'gait' when not referring to something swinging on a fence?

I'm learning.

That's not right. You're still a kid. Dad's a decent man. Our grandfather is an evil influence on you, I say.

Have you seen him diabolic?

There you go again, and yes, look at his legs, they're fine and aren't supposed to be.

We gaze at the Old Fiend's trousers. Polly scribbles something in her sketchpad. My grandfather drops the stone. It lands an inch or two from the squirrel. He says, All right, Peter, raise it from the dead, nods to Polly; they shuffle back inside conspiratorially.

I spend some time trying to recall Peter. No bells ring. I glance up at the nest that looks like a hat the Green Giant might wear. I don't get any advice from above. Trees have been deleafed. Winter's encroaching. Bordt's Potato Chips smell ominous in the half-light.

In the garage I find a Frisbee. When I roll the squirrel onto the disk I want to believe it moves on its own. There isn't any blood underneath, on the driveway. I take it to my room. I lock the door. I try to feed it orange juice from a little dropper. Its whiskers get sticky. I pet its head and steal a peek at the teeth. I begin to enjoy the squirrel's company. We play a little Atari, I help him with the joystick. I mention Amy Cowser and her big 'ole glasses. The squirrel grins. I get tired of thinking of it as "the squirrel" so I name him Rodney. I promise never to say Rod. My parents call me down for dinner. I wash up. Nobody says anything about anything. Dad keeps passing and repassing me the salt. My grandfather and sister take turns whispering about the weather, how it's supposed to snow. I can't eat quick enough. My Mom cares about my homework; I excuse myself to not do it.

Rodney and I share a few more laughs, but then, just like that, he starts to stink. Things are turning serious, I think. Maybe the smell is me. I say a prayer before bed: *Dear God, bring Rodney back, take Old Hodge away.* I can't sleep for a while so I count sheep until they turn into squirrels.

In the morning Rodney's missing. I think maybe he's gone to Heaven, but that's silly. At the breakfast table are pancakes and my family. I ask the obvious.

I threw that stinking thing away when I got back from work last night, my father says. What were you doing with it in your room, Tiger?

I make the mistake of mentioning Rodney when I say I was trying to nurse it back to health.

You named it? my sister asks happily.

Dad passes me the syrup. Old Hodge grins. Mom is concerned about rabies. I try to make it no big deal.

I'll tell you what, Old Hodge says, while you're at school, I'll dig it out of the trash, lop the tail off, and sew it onto one of your baseball caps. You'll be just like

Daniel Boone.

The table laughs. I tell him to go to hell, in my napkin.

School yields. I'm disappointed to find it snowing afterwards. The hat is on my bed with Rodney's tail. I don't know where he got the thread or the needle. Nobody thinks I'll wear it, but I do. Everyday. And I read the Bible. I suppose Old Hodge isn't as bad as Satan after all. That doesn't mean I like sharing his name. Then he dies of the shakes in April. I take the hat off and go out the front door again.

I convince Jed to call me Mark. I explain that a house divided against itself cannot stand. This doesn't make sense to him, but it does to me. For my birthday I get a golden cross and a chain from my parents. I decide to forgive my Dad for cheating if that's what he has been doing. I'm trying to live more deliberately. I tell my sister I'm sorry about the scar on her forehead. She says, No big deal, we were both young. I say, But still. She says she's sorry about Rodney, she'll be sad when Fatso dies. I make a mental note to stop over-feeding the gerbil when she isn't around just to watch those tiny cheeks puff out.

Trees turn green. It seems to me most people don't notice leaves when a tree is full, just the green. That summer, riding my bike, after Hodge was gone, I had my head up hunting for the perfect leaf—shaped just right, verdant, blemishless—so I could watch it develop, turn, speckle, wilt, collapse, fall and catch in Autumn; when I ran into a pole, fell off my bike, twisted my legs. It was no big deal. Nobody saw me. I limped for a couple of weeks. When high school rolled around my legs were fine, really, but every time I crouch down now my knees make this uncomfortable-sounding pop and people look at me as if I should be in pain. I want to tell them that I'm all right. It doesn't hurt at all.

Des

Arghh, I say, into the microphone, trying to sound con-
vincing. A-hoy, Mateys, let's blast them Tigers out of
their hides!

I fire the cannon, Kaboom. The crowd flinches their
shoulders in surprise; a few children cover their ears.
A man wearing green applauds. The crowd erupts into
cheers. Everybody loves football. I say some fiery words
into the microphone. My wife, in the bleachers, looks
uncomfortable on those metal bench-seats. I am on a
makeshift boat wearing a patch and a bandana. I am a pirate, we are the Pirates. My son is on the sidelines where
he will be the entire game. He's wearing a baseball hat
backwards because he has no real need for a helmet. The
coach never plays him. My daughter is in the car in part
because of the black cat, I think. I'm not sure about this.
She's a tough nut to crack. MaryLou asked me a week
ago, in what I want to believe was the waning stage of
our affair, If the apocalypse was now but you and someone could be saved, who'd you choose?

Right.

The Glee Club made this boat, happily. It's pretty

sturdy. There is a mast rising from the center of it with rungs. At the top of the mast is a circular platform large enough for a small brass cannon with a big punch, a microphone with a long cord running to a generator down on deck, me, gun powder, and a fancy silver lighter with an engraved beaver on it. My teeth are large and friends have pointed it out. I keep the lighter in my breast pocket and am quick to light whatever is necessary. I have baggy pants and am overweight. They like me this way, the principal and coaches, but I refuse to grow a bushy beard. I told my superiors that I wouldn't be trivialized by traditional pirates, Blue Beard, Black Toes, whatever. I am simply myself, but a pirate. My family talked about names over dinner tonight before the game. We were eating chicken; overcooked chicken, not that I could do better, I couldn't, I've scorched soup. My son said Moses. He has turned religious since his grandfather died. My daughter said Des. Des, the Pirate. I had no idea what that meant. She's a tough nut to crack. My wife said she was filing for a divorce. I told her that name was too long. What about just Dan, my name, Dan the Pirate, or Pirate Dan Meanus? I passed the salt to my son, the chicken needed something.

I am not a mascot full-time. I own a cigar shop downtown. I've saved enough money to make a commercial this winter. I have an idea for one: *Meanus, Meanus, Meanus Cigars, the meanest cigars in the whole damn town! Meanus with a junk-yard dog, Meanus with old King Kong!* I don't know. I may borrow the pirate get-up and wear the patch. The patch was my idea in the first place, it isn't one of the requirements. The principal, a woman without much of a mouth, told me the patch would impede my vision and I would topple from the mast and break my neck. She would not be responsible. I signed something in accordance.

I became the mascot out of desperation. My family has been falling apart. I can't relate to my kids. Well, my son is pretty normal, I suppose, but my daughter is a tough nut to crack. And there's the wife problem. I've been having trouble getting it up. We score, I Arghh, Kaboom. The crowd cringes again, but not my wife, she saw it coming. She works at Bordt's Potato Chip Factory, I know the owner, Bordt, he's a fine man. I tried blaming my wife, mentioned that I can't make love when she smells like Sour Cream and Onions, or Barbecue. They're making Ketchup-flavored chips now but nobody is supposed to know this. It's a campaign secret, a marketing strategy. I asked Polly, my wife, about it. She wouldn't budge, but you can't lie about your odor. I told her Ketchup had no business in the bedroom. She made some snide comment about how I'd rarely been around, how denial didn't get me any harder, I didn't smell so great myself, nag, nag, nag. These things, of course, were true.

The Pirates try to run the option. It works, we score again, I fire the cannon. There aren't any balls in the thing, it's just gun powder and blanks. Below me I see girls twirling batons in scarlet tights. The band plays a fight song, the trumpet is off. I start a chant, into the microphone: Go Pirates, go. Go Pirates, go. Go Pirates, go. Mouths open and close.

Polly, my daughter, is in the car. She's named after my wife, obviously. This gets confusing so I call her PieDoll. My daughter, that is. I just call my wife Polly. We've never had pet-names. I should give her one maybe, could spice things up in the bedroom. My son, Hodge, is named after my wife's father. I haven't been one to argue, but he should have been named after me. Danny, Dan Jr. (D.J.), Daniel the Second. Something honoring the father. I call him Tiger because when he was younger he was a scrapper. We're playing the Tigers today, so I won't be calling him that now. Could call him Des, Jr. Young Pirate Des? Sure don't know where PieDoll comes up with things.

My daughter is in the car because she crossed a black cat the other day before it was hit by our neighbor's car. She's convinced she is bad luck. She didn't cry and doesn't. Not even about the divorce. My son sobbed a little about that, thankfully. I told him there-there. Then we arrived at school. Polly said she was staying in the car, we were all doomed. She is in the backseat of our cream-colored car, passenger side. My wife slammed the door a little when she got out. Hodge hustled to the field for high-fives and the bench. I put my patch on and climbed to my roost, sullen.

My daughter is probably staring at the headrest in front of her in the empty car. She is counting to some specific number like fifty-five and then counting back to zero. She'll skip the number three because she doesn't like it. Her hands are in her lap. If there were an apocalypse and I could save someone else it would be Polly, my daughter. Practically, she's youngest and has the most life ahead of her. When she grows out of her bad luck phase she will do something important. She's bright. She once did a project on bees for her science class. The bees flew in concentric circles by her whim. They did tricks. One of the rowdy bees stung her on a cloudy afternoon. She had opened her umbrella by accident in our foyer that morning. It just popped open. Polly is smarter than me, she's over my head, and I seem to miss things. She came home from school and mentioned the sting. I found the tiny stinger and tweezed it out. What else could I do? I told her it was just nature, or something.

She said, Bad luck.

I said, O.K., yeah, the umbrella this morning, but you're fine, aren't you PieDoll?

Not bad luck for me, she said, bad luck for the bees. The bee died, that's what they do after they sting. Besides, she said, I was angry and killed them all with a nasty insecticide. I was bad luck for them.

A hand-off to number twenty-five, Alvin Hoagie, he sweeps around the outside, breaks a tackle and scores, Kaboom; nobody flinches. I say into the microphone, Go Pirates, go. Go Pirates, go. My son scowls up at me.

What? I say into the microphone, to him.

He quickly turns around. It would be nice if his coach, Zan, was sleeping with my wife. Once, she made cookies for the team. Oatmeal, I believe. Zan nearly ate them all. She didn't mind, even pointed out a crumb on his lip. It's not that I want my wife to be boinking the coach; I just think maybe we'd be even that way. I would feel better about MaryLou.

I met MaryLou at my cigar shop, almost two years ago. I don't smoke cigars myself, I just like the smell from other peoples' mouths. She bought a real whopper from Honduras, eight years old. I lit it up for her right there in the store. She introduced herself as Mary, mumble. She mumbles. She meant MaryLou, I learned later.

Dan Meanus, how do you do?

I offered my hand for the shaking. She was working the cigar in her right hand so she stuck out her left hand. I took it with my left hand and mid-shake she placed her pinky on my wedding ring. She mumbled something smoky.

Yeah, I said, yeah, I got one of them.

It, the relationship, evolved. I don't dance and we went dancing. I like her a lot and deny it. There's no other choice. MaryLou always understands. No pressure. She's got glasses and bobbed hair. She is not too-thin and doesn't seem concerned. I know she is smarter than me. She graduated from college and is a conversationalist. She allows me to think out loud. She'd make a fine psychologist but she works for a law firm. She doesn't smell like anything but herself. We've done seventy-percent of the hotels in this town, almost always in the daytime. She said maybe she'd show up to the game later to see me in my cute uniform. I started to tell her No, my wife, but confrontation between them might help me sort things out somehow. If my wife turned psycho on MaryLou it would show she cared. MaryLou cares, I know, she chooses her undergarments to my liking, but I've let things come too far. I started a family, I want to finish it.

Pass to number eighty-eight Todd Friddle, touchdown, Kaboom, Go Pirates, go. Hodge, keep your chin up, son!

My son looks at the ground, I think, I just see his back, his shoulders slump.

It's all right, Tig! Zan, play my son. This could be a chant, I realize. Zan, play my son. Zan, play my son. Zan, play my son. The crowd doesn't participate. A man in a green shirt applauds. Our team is winning handily so people ignore me and focus on our good fortune. Half-time passes. The damned trumpet. I click the microphone off. If my wife had a rifle, and aim, the situation would unfold differently. As is, she seems to be willing me to fall from my perch.

I told my wife about the affair, finally. I sort of thought she knew, but she acted surprised. Like acting surprised about a funeral, I mean, come on, you know he's dead, the funeral part doesn't just sneak up on you. She lost her father, a nervous man who stared, a couple of years ago. We were late to the funeral because Polly, my wife, was cross-stitching in the foyer. I said, Hello, we've got some place to be. Let's get moving. She wept. She was the only one. My son sobbed a little bit, but nothing big. My daughter drew a picture in her sketchpad; I peeked and noticed she was drawing our family. I had huge brown ears. Then we went home and had tea. My wife didn't want to talk about it, just stitch. She is taller than me by an inch and younger than me by four years. She is thin with thick hair and the reason our daughter is beautiful. Our son, like me, is timid and pudgy. My wife practices some form of karate I can't pronounce and it hurts. I thought maybe she was stitching some funeral shawl because all the yarn was black, but when she was done she just tossed it over the birdcage so our nervous bird Skinny could sleep at night.

I'm not going to fall, I say, but the microphone is off. I'm thinking about clicking it on and giving her a piece of my mind when the crowd thunders. I turn back to the game. We've scored, Jed Jr. on a reverse. I Arghh, but forget the microphone is off. I click it on, Arghh. This comes late, people notice. Go, Pirates go. Go, Pirates go. Go, Pirates go. They realize my cheer is uneasy. It seems simple, just express commendation when something good happens to our team. The principal wasn't going to let me be the mascot at first. She said someone jollier should do the job. I wanted to bring the family unit together through sport so I begged her to let me give it a try anyway. I told her I used to be a male cheerleader for my high school which is something I don't mention often. Besides, my voice is deep like a pirate. I snap the microphone off and tell myself to do better.

The black cat came around purring and hungry. My son fed it tuna and talked to it. Polly named it something like Tweeker. They got to know the thing. Then it occurred to Polly that Tweeker didn't have a single spot on her and was thereby solid black and bad news. She avoided it when it came around. Hodge grew bored of it, distracted by his awkward body, his ghoulish pimples, his tummy rolls. Walking home from the bus stop a couple of days ago Polly saw Tweeker sleeping under a tree. She passed the cat on the sidewalk, crossed it, so to speak. Tweeker was hit by my neighbor's car yesterday and we found out about it before dinner this evening. I saw Jed cleaning it from his Volvo grill. He was whistling a western tune until I approached him and then he tried to look somber.

Tweeker?

Damned thing just seemed to fall from the sky.

More likely a tree.

Yeah. I heard you've been sleeping around.

Yeah, you?

Jed chuckled and hit me in the shoulder. Sure hope we stomp them Tigers. Jed Jr.'s going to be returning kicks, playing wide receiver, covering for Jo-Jo Jr. at free safety...

Oh, yeah? Jed wasn't done.

I wasn't done.

My apologies.

Gonna fill in as tackle, nose-guard, might be back-up to Brady at quarterback...

Her name is MaryLou, she has a perfect nose.

I figure he'll put in about twenty-one, maybe twenty-eight points tonight.

I think I'm falling in love with this woman, finally, which isn't at all what I want and something I can't rationalize, not that I'm the type that needs to rationalize my affair to you, Jed, you killed a cat and probably will screw up my daughter's sense of self.

Just between you and me, Danny, I've introduced my son to steroids.

I tried to tell my family about Tweeker before dinner. The chicken was already overcooked and they were sitting. My son sobbed a little. My daughter didn't seem too surprised. Then we tried to name me as Pirate. Des, I guess. Certainly not Moses, I can't even part my hair neatly.

I think that I'd not take myself if there were an apocalypse. I'd give that space to MaryLou. She and my daughter. They would make a good mother/daughter duo. Polly needs someone to challenge her, God knows I've failed in that regard, and my wife has just seemed sad ever since her father died. I'm sure my affair hasn't helped her out of the funk. I've told MaryLou everything about my daughter, they are similar in their confident demeanor. Both of them have a quiet smile that sharpens their eyes. They have identical laughs. I imagine them chuckling lightly over a black-and-white movie nobody understands. Let them be saved, I'll take my wife and son, embrace them and lift my chin to Kingdom Come.

I catch my wife looking at me. Ah-ha! I say, clicking on the microphone. She stares at her knees. I saw that, there was longing in that look, Polly. Sweetheart.

A man in a green shirt applauds.

Jed, in the audience, tells me to shut-up, his son just made an interception. Actually he says, Hey, shut-up you dumb-ass pirate, my son just picked one off.

This is problematic, me being a dumb-ass pirate. That's no name.

My name is Des, Jed, Des the pirate. Call me that. By the way, you make a lousy father.

People in the crowd turn to Jed. He's red. You make a lousy husband, Des, he shouts.

The crowd volleys their attention to my perch. I shift weight from foot to foot. I Arghh, fire the cannon, Kaboom. This surprises them, distracts, shoulders lift. But not Jed, he isn't done.

Des the Pirate, that's desperate. We've got a desperate man for our team mascot. That's fitting considering fatso up there.

The crowd erupts in laughter. Jed gives someone a high-five and starts a Des, Des, Des, chant. The bleachers rock. This stings, coming from my daughter and all. She had to know what the name meant. It isn't nice to call your father a name he doesn't even know he's being called. It's cruel. I'll have to talk to her about it. I know I've been absent from her life. She certainly deserves better than me. In an ideal world MaryLou would convince her that I was a decent man. I'd patch things up with the wife. Then MaryLou could bring the respectful Piedoll back to the family. We'd thank MaryLou as she drove away and always think of her fondly. My wife and I could refer to these times as the Turbulent Years that made our marriage stronger. The chanting crowd is loud enough to reach the parking lot where my daughter might hear and feel ashamed.

My son, on the sidelines, has sympathy in his eyes,

God love him. My wife picks up her pocket book and starts on down the stands. She doesn't look at me. The crowd stomps their feet.

Yeah, sure, I'm desperate, but I'm up here trying, aren't I? I'm supporting the team. I'm not afraid to admit that I've made some mistakes. I love my wife and family. Maybe my daughter might be better suited elsewhere. I've found a woman who might make a difference.

Nobody is listening to me. The crowd has gotten into a zone. My wife is having trouble getting out. Somebody starts a wave and it works. People go this way and that way. I'm getting seasick watching. I'm sure it's against protocol, but I turn the cannon around and aim it at Jed. He is less red now. I have no idea how our team is doing. I fire the cannon at him, symbolically, of course, there aren't any balls, Kaboom. He flinches and colors again. Take that, Kaboom. The wave pauses momentarily.

MaryLou appears by the stairs. She's picked a fine time to show up. My wife freezes not far from her. I guess she just knows. Something passes between them. I fire the cannon at Jed again. I mention that he's pathetic. Everyone hears. The wave breaks up, the chant turns to just loud mumbling. I hear a child say not to point that thing at him. He has a lot of growing up to do. My wife is moving toward MaryLou. Jed is angrily stepping over people to the boat. The game goes on. We're late in the fourth quarter. People are filing out into the aisles and following Jed down the bleachers. They come two by two.

My wife approaches MaryLou. They are standing close to one another with folded arms. The fence between the stands and the field falls under the weight of the oncoming crowd. They are rushing my boat. My wife untucks an arm and I wonder if she is going to karate-chop MaryLou. She doesn't, scratches her nose. They shake hands. I fire up the microphone.

Polly, Buttercup, it's not her fault. I'm the one to blame, I'm bad. I want us to work this out, regardless. Let's not make this a total waste. I take out my car keys and fling them at MaryLou. They arc over the crowd and land near my wife's feet. Not a bad pass. My son is looking up at me, or, maybe more correctly, gazing past me on up into the blue yonder. I'm proud of him for being a trooper. Jed is on deck, others are not far behind. Our team is still scoring viciously. It's got to be over soon. The trumpeter is tone-deaf.

Pick up the keys, MaryLou. Take them and go to the parking lot. Look for the cream-colored sedan with the little girl in the backseat. It's near the tennis courts. She's our daughter. Take her away, she'll like you, just be yourself.

The microphone is yanked out of my hands by someone below. It squeals all the way down and when it lands the din is amplified. A group of kids find it and start saying, Fuck, fuck, fuck, happily. They giggle. My wife picks up the keys. MaryLou refolds her arms. Jed is coming up here to kick my ass. There isn't enough room for that. The boat is teetering. I fire the cannon because it seems right to do, Kaboom.

My wife and MaryLou are discussing something. Is MaryLou laughing? Give her the keys, Polly, there's no time! Without the microphone, I cannot be heard. I lose sight of them. The patch is impeding my vision.

Jed climbs to the top of the perch and punches me in the mouth. He is bigger than me, this will be easy for him. He cracks me in the chin. The crowd erupts into cheers. I don't know if our team just scored again or if they are glad I'm getting beat up.

I do the unexpected. I leap up into Jed's arms. He doesn't want me there. We are unsteady on his feet. He whispers for me to get down, we'll fall like this.

I take my patch off and see that my wife is standing alone. Her arms are folded. She untucks them. I wonder if she is going to give me the finger. She puts her hand to her lips and blows me a kiss.

I reach out for it, a chance.

Terrified by Raisins

From my place on the grainy preschool linoleum I spied
Barry Johnson creeping over to Thomas. He carried a
straw plugged at each end by his thumbs. The straw
had a red line worming around the plastic where you
put your mouth, like a thin tongue. He had ticks in the
straw, having gathered them from the playground wood-
pile, I suppose. The straw fit nicely into Thomas's ear,
he was sleeping, it was nap-time, teach was smoking,
away. Barry blew into the straw, blew the lot of ticks into
Thomas's brain (later they used a curiously large pair of
tweezers, I wondered what they used them for besides
ripping ticks from a child's skull, and still, hell, you yank
a tick and the head stays in there, nasty things that they
are, did they get them all?). Thomas awoke and swatted
Barry, the straw fell from his ear with three ticks, like
little drops of chocolate, onto the cold floor.

In a children's book I read that ticks infest man. I didn't
know what infest meant, so I looked it up, but I was
distracted by homologous and hotsy-totsy; years later I
was homologous with a woman who told me everything

rested in detail, which I believe is a lie. Show me the detail of pain, loneliness, love; you distasteful strumpet!

On the veranda Thomas and I played dominoes until our ears rang with cicada-buzz, evening. We'd line them up and down the stairs and zigzag across the lacquered wooden slats, Thomas so steady with his hands. I always insisted on tipping the whole affair, and they fell, like the balance of our youth, laboriously.

I turned adult. Infest means to be parasitic in or on. I am insured, I sleep with ear-plugs, I am terrified by raisins, I disappear when you aren't thinking about it. I go to McKinley's Wharf when I have time, now. I'm there listening to vulgar boatmen, my head infested with opinion. The sky, sea, etc.; all blue. A pal of mine mentions that it is his ambition in life to die penniless in a desert. He's been drinking, and I order him something sweet because that sounds all right. Sand and sun, empty sleeves, empty pockets; unflinching everything.

I recall a game of Red Rover. Everyone was there, Thomas and I held hands, I was on the end. So happens Barry Johnson was called out (he had an enormous head like a plum). He came at Thomas and me, meaning to break through our chain. Something moved between us, we weren't letting go, not like that. It mattered and it didn't because that son-of-a-bitch ran into me full-tilt and half the line toppled over onto the sun-blanched grass.

Scarecrowed

Bud, Nadine, and I move slowly toward Tritch's farm to watch the annual scarecrow contest. I don't mind our pace, I'm not in a hurry, it is November and I feel as if I'm on the edge of discovering something.

I found Bud under a population sign a few months ago. Nine hundred and sixty-five people, and Bud. He's a swell guy, short; maybe a midget. His face is big compared to his body, you can't miss it. I've seen coconuts wash up on the shores of Florida with black eye-pits that look like Bud. His skin is orange or appears so because of his red hair. He doesn't speak. I wouldn't say he's mute, I've heard him whistle, I just don't think he has much to talk about. He introduced himself with a business card that read: *Bud-Exterminator Extraordinare*. Some sort of bug had been mashed onto the back of the card and he carried two small metallic canisters with hoses. Nadine was becoming a handful, Bud was wayward; bingo, a match. He could help me be Nadine's keeper.

Tritch's farm grows mostly wheat and vegetables. One of the corn fields is fallow and that's where people are setting up their scarecrows. There are rules hand-painted on an old wagon: *Each scarecrow must be five yards from another scarecrow, no tampering, if a crow alights you lose, over at sunset.* We didn't enter the contest, but I know Nadine enjoys watching anyway.

Mr. Tritch gives a speech: Good to see all you boys, and ladies, nice out her t'day, scary scarecrows, woo. Dig in to them worms. A cow-licked boy uncovers a wash basin full of earthworms and a crowd of beaming children advance. Bud looks at me dolefully, wanting to join the children but reluctant to leave Nadine.

Go on, I'll watch her, I say. Bud skips away, his head a'cant. Children grab handfuls of worms, sprint into the field, fling them on the ground, at the scarecrows, over each other.

I negotiate Nadine through the gathering crowd. A few people nod at us. Nadine is my mother who stroked a half-year ago. She was in the kitchen struggling to open a bag of Fruities when she hollered, collapsed. I had been upstairs on my bed doing whatever. She'd managed 911 by the time I found her there on the linoleum tile twitching. I pounded on her chest and became fascinated with the jiggle of her breasts, hypnotic, really. Ambulances came, took her away, told me I'd done good, stabilized her. She was wheel-chaired and can now do nothing more than blurt on occasion and shake. She can feel too, I know. I dropped out of school to take care of her. The neighborhood found me endearing, a hero of sorts. They caught me patting Nadine's head in a newspaper picture. Nadine was staring right at the camera with sky-cloudy eyes.

At first, just after the stroke, Nadine was bitter and purposefully soiled herself. I talked to her about it. I mentioned the bit about lemons and lemonade. I'd comb her hair with a fancy silver brush she kept in her boudoir—hell, it's more just a closet with a mirror, but she used to like it there. I tried leaving her in the bathroom where I'd installed metal bars to help her move from the wheelchair to the toilet after doctors said she had regained some faculties in her arms. When I retrieved her I'd find a defiant wet spot on her blue- or yellow-flowered dress, in a formaldehyde-smelling daze. Sometimes she'd be in tears she was too stubborn to wipe away.

And then, Bud. The moment I brought him home, Nadine straightened up. The two of them communicate with their eyes somehow. I smell perfume on her from time to time. Bud whistles to her out on the porch, and she tries to whistle back. I've heard her make little noises, but mostly just spit. I've allowed Bud to move from his makeshift room in the basement up to the couch in the living room. Nadine's bedroom is nearby, and if she happens to need him in the night, there he is. As far as I know Bud hasn't attempted to get an exterminating job and has become, for the most part, a freeloader. He cooks, cleans, watches Nadine, and for this I allow him to stay. We get insurance checks from Nadine's accident and from my father who left but sends money every month in cards that explain his love.

Bud returns with a grin. I see a worm working its way through the red curls of his hair. It must be wet on his scalp.

Let me get that, I say.

It's the adults' turn to toss worms. I figure I'll go ahead. Bud's got his eye on Nadine.

At the worm basin I see Emily Hunter. She is my next-door neighbor. She is my age, about seventeen. She dropped out of high school too although I don't know why. She works for a company that manufactures red and white striped mints. She is Ms. Hunter's daughter. Ms. Hunter is a knockout, the type of woman who looks fine in a storm. I've peeped Ms. Hunter on plenty of occasions, her bedroom is adjacent to mine. I have a pair of small binoculars. I don't see her now.

Emily is deep in the worms and I find a place next to her. I say hello, comment on the day, mention that a plate of spaghetti would hit the spot. I'm being coy.

She acknowledges this by locking her pinky around mine. I take her hand, in the worms, and match my breathing with hers. She's a pretty girl. Besides, someday she might look like her mother.

Hey, Scottie, someone says behind me.

That's me, although I prefer Scott.

Hey, what? I say and turn, Emily turns with me, our hands release; damn.

A man in a red-black-white flannel shirt over overalls with mascara and a straw hat tells me that Frank is ill, they need another scarecrow-man, would I oblige?

Emily puts her arm around my shoulder and obliges on my behalf. She is having fun with me and I don't mind.

Instructions are: *Take this yellow flag, raise it slowly if a crow alights on a nearby scarecrow to alert the panel of judges. If a crow alights on you, shoo it by blowing gently, wear a scarecrowy outfit, put on mascara.* Emily applies the mascara. She stands close enough for me to smell her minty breath, her breasts brush my arm three times which is really all it takes for me to fall in love.

Go get 'em Mr. Scarecrow, Emily says.

I'm only doing this for you, I reply, taking her hand, kissing it even, Mrs. Scarecrow.

I make my way through the crowd which mildly applauds me. I pass Bud and Nadine who seem happy. Bud shrugs, I shrug back. I pass a table with three judges sitting on fold-out chairs, scorecards in place. They look the same, stern and androgynous. One judge nods. I nod back. On the table is a picture of a green tractor which is the prize for scariest scarecrow. I walk out into the field, obliterating worms as I go, knowing that Emily has her eyes on me.

The sky is bespeckeled with blackbirds. There is a scarecrow to my right which is wearing a pin-striped suit and a tie. Unlike the other scarecrows, this one is bare-headed, shameless under God, a newspaper tucked under one of his arms. This is the work of a disgruntled businessman-turned-farmer out in the crowd. If he wins, he will drive his green tractor into the city and park it in rush-hour traffic, sit on his upraised mushroom-shaped seat, and jeer at the world. If he doesn't win, his suit will be riddled with crow shit and when his farm fails and he returns to business, he will be a mess. Either way, the scarecrow is staring at me, and I feel a bit uncomfortable.

I have time to think, standing like I am. *Yellow flag, crow on scarecrow down in front. I wonder about Mr. Hunter.* He's absent. *Yellow flag, crow on scarecrow with sunglasses and turban.* My father is gone too, tired of Nadine. It would be nice if Mr. Hunter and my father were bank robbers in Arizona wearing cowboy hats, spurs, red-and-white bandannas triangled over nose and mouth saying "stick em up" in grave, muffled low-voices. *Yellow flag, crow on imitation Boone scarecrow with coon-cap.* Of course, they'd get gunned down somewhere outside of Tucson in a shootout with the law, leaving no traces of booty. *Shoo crow.* One day I'd get a mysterious letter in the mail that just had, "Take five paces east from the cactus that looks like a hand without a thumb at mile-marker 135 off Highway 66," written on it, and, "I always loved you, son." *Yellow flag, crow on scarecrow with fishing rod.* And Emily would reveal that she too had a mysterious letter that read, "After the five paces, take another eight paces north where you'll see a boot sticking out of the desert. Dig, my dear Emily, dig four or five feet, and know I love you forever!" We'd piece the notes together and go, go, go. *Yellow flag, crow on business scarecrow with shit-stained suit.*

The next day I am at the Hunter's house cutting the grass. No one has asked me to do this, but it feels like the thing to do. The yard is mostly brittle leaves and weeds and does not require much effort. I have enough hair on my chest to remove my shirt, but I'm having trouble working up a sweat. So far, nothing from inside; the Hunters could be at church, at a state fair, visiting relatives in town. I just know they're not home.

Bud ambles over and follows me around, tugging at my trousers. He is mouthing something, trying to communicate, but I refuse to turn off the lawnmower and his lips are too small to read. If the Hunters see me with him, I don't know what they will think. I don't know exactly where Bud fits into my family.

He disappears by the time I reach the front yard. I finish and return the lawnmower to our garage. A thin trace of grass lingers on the driveway. I kick at it with my sneakers which is useless; it remains.

Inside, I write, *Compliments of Mr. Scarecrow*, on a piece of paper. Bud is sitting Indian-style on the kitchen counter twiddling his thumbs, eyebrows twitching. When I start to ask him what his problem is, he switches directions with his thumbs and thumps them together. I tell him I don't need this child's play.

Outside the sun is behind clouds and the wind has picked up. The trace of grass is gone. My skin is prickling but I am reluctant to put my shirt on just yet. I knock on the Hunters' door. When nobody answers I stick the note under the brass knocker and leave.

A boy on a blue dirt-bike snickers from the sidewalk. His name is Chad Turner, he lives down the block. When I approach him, he rides off. I follow him four houses down to a group of middle-schoolers huddled around a younger child clutching Matchbox cars to his chest. Other cars litter the driveway. When I get close to the boys, Chad whispers something to them and points at me. I put my shirt on.

Scottie's in love with Easy Emily, Chad taunts, and repeats himself. The others turn their attention from the child to me.

I tell him to call me Scott.

I saw you cutting her lawn with a swagger, Chad says, and the other boys stand behind him.

I mention that he doesn't know what a swagger is.

You're trying to get a piece of her like Davey Ward did, Chad says.

Davey Ward plays for the high school soccer team. I have heard he beats his dog.

I bet she'll get pregnant again, one of the boys states.

I ask if he is implying that Davey Ward impregnated Emily.

Him or Michael Hoag porked her, a different boy

chides. A wave of giggles ensues.

Michael Hoag wrestles.

Your mom or midget-father better have a few hundred bucks to pay for another abortion, Chad says.

I realize the situation has gotten out of hand. I shove Chad and his blue bike to the ground. The boys are hesitant, I know they'll attack me if I let them. I grab a Matchbox car from the driveway. It is a van, actually, with bubble windows. I think about chucking it at Chad, but decide to aim for a streetlight above us. The boys are distracted. I pick up a yellow corvette and throw it at the light again. The boys catch on. Chad picks himself up and bikes away, he has a skinned knee. The child starts to howl as the boys pry cars from his hands and toss them at the streetlight. Soon the sky is filled with Matchbox cars, like errant satellites.

I return to the house without a swagger. Bud is in the boudoir massaging Nadine's knees. I sit on the couch in the living room. The day slips away. Bud takes Nadine for a walk. When I hear a soft knock on the door I do not trust myself to answer it.

At night I decide to peep on the Hunters. Nadine is already tucked away in her bedroom, and Bud has been hovering around me with anticipation in his eyes. He may be concerned for me, I have been quiet and won't acknowledge him. I mention that I am going out for some air and for him not to follow me. I slam the door for emphasis.

There is no moon outside and streetlights have been broken by boys with good aim. I find a light on in Emily's room. She is inside jump-roping in front of a large oval mirror. There is a dresser and a chair in the corner. Her hair is up, twisted, and I can see the pink nape of her neck perspiring. I think I hear Mozart on her stereo and this makes her jumping seem elegant. I believe these are her pajamas, soft-yellow cotton shorts with matching top, no bra. Her breasts are small enough to remain under control with motion. The carpet on the floor is worn from her short jumps. I imagine her feet are callused. If she had an abortion it shouldn't matter. I wonder who the lousy father was?

I wait until her rhythm breaks and she stops, turns the stereo off, slips into bed, extinguishes the light. I return home with an enormous weight on my shoulders.

In the morning, on my way to Davey Ward's house, I pass a flatbed, a flat-tired trike, and a green-lustered penny which I ignore.

Mrs. Ward tells me Davey is out back. There is a German Shepherd and a chessboard on the back porch. Davey and I play, the dog snarls. Davey beats me in fifteen moves, he points out; mate. I ask him if he deflowered Emily. He says no, why? I tell him no reason.

On my way to Michael Hoag's house I pass a garden full of periwinkles and chattahoochee slabs. Mrs. Hoag tells me Michael is in the basement making paper animals.

I ask if she means origami.

She is slightly cross-eyed. Paper animals, she says again.

Michael is working on a paper butterfly in the basement, under a halogen lamp, in tight white underwear. There is a stack of colorful square pieces of paper in front of him. He tells me to give it a try. I take a blue piece of paper and fold it until it looks like folded blue paper. He wants me to try again. I find a purple piece of paper and he puts his hands on mine, works my fingers. I ask if he deflowered Emily.

He is confused by the word.

I explain that I mean bop and impregnate.

He says no, and squeezes my hands tightly. He is strong and could easily pin me. The purple piece of paper turns into a lop-sided pair of lips. He asks me if I enjoy papier-mâché. I don't know where he's going with that question. He asks if I would spar with him for a while and I quietly excuse myself, leaving my lips in the basement.

Back home I find Bud in the boudoir trying to hump Nadine. His pants are around his ankles and Nadine's stockings are at her feet. Bud is having trouble straddling the wheelchair and sticking his small penis into Nadine's static and cottony organ. For all of their effort, they are still smiling, not getting anything done.

Bud, I say, get off.

I startle him, he jumps from the wheelchair, adjusts his pants, stands in front of her.

We're in love, Bud says. This is the first thing that I've ever heard him say, and it is quiet enough for it to be my imagination.

Huh? I say.

She and me are in love, Bud repeats with a tinny sing-song voice. We've been trying to tell you.

You should have tried harder. I didn't see this coming.

Nadine is slack-jawed with steady eyes. Her legs are apart with Bud between them protecting her sex. It is difficult for me to see her this way.

This isn't decent, I say.

I want to marry her, Bud sing-songs. His head is

twitching and looks uncomfortable.

No, I say, how are you going to support her?

I'll kill bugs again.

Your canisters are empty.

I can refill them, I know some people.

I won't have you as a father.

You don't have to call me Dad.

Marrying her makes you him, regardless. I won't have that. Get out of the house, Bud.

I notice Nadine struggling with her arms, flapping them, really. She moves her mouth open and shut collecting saliva at the corners. Bud reaches up and places his hand on her cheek, behind an ear. He climbs up on her chair, careful not to expose anything, and makes soft cooing sounds. Nadine continues mouthing. She is trying to say something to me, but I won't read her lips. Her eyes are clear enough. They say, *Son, I'll kill you.*

I leave the house with a chip on my shoulder. I will go next door to face Emily, ask her about the abortion and just get over it.

Ms. Hunter answers the door and my determination falters. This is a woman with control. She leads me into the kitchen, pours a glass of lemonade, beckons Emily, and excuses herself to run some errands. In motion, she is exquisite.

Emily enters the kitchen in a blue tee-shirt and miniskirt. She has freckles I hadn't noticed.

Hi, Scott, she says.

Hi, Emily, I return.

She sits on a stool and positions her legs where I can try to follow them up her skirt. It occurs to me that I could feel if she's had an abortion, I wouldn't have to ask her, there might be scars down there or something.

Thanks for cutting our grass, she says.

It was nothing.

How's your mom?

Fine, fine.

Want to smoke some weed?

Sure.

Emily leads me down a hallway and into her bedroom. I carry my lemonade. She walks a little flat-footed, but with a similar hip-swishing technique like her mother. She closes the door in her room. I stare at the worn space on the carpet where she's been jump-roping. She pulls weed from her bottom drawer, when she bends I catch a glimpse of flowered panties. As she stands up, I glare at the carpet. She sits on the bed and rolls a joint.

Sit down, she says.

I sit on the chair by the dresser. There is a picture of a man holding a baby on a bookshelf next to the dresser. It is quiet, I can hear children rough-housing somewhere in the neighborhood. She passes the joint, I take a hit and pass it back.

What do you think of Bud? I ask.

Who?

Bud, you know, the short silent guy, big face.

Oh, yeah. He seems nice. What does he do?

She smokes and passes.

Not much, I manage. I smoke, pass back. Tell me about your father.

He's dead, Emily says.

Oh, I'm sorry.

What about yours? Emily asks.

He's a bank robber.

Emily chokes on smoke and passes the joint to me.

That's what I like about you, she says, you say the

oddest things.

I nod into the joint. When I finish, I pass it back to her and slide onto the bed. While she takes another hit, I place my hand on her knees.

What's this? she asks, teasingly.

I think you're beautiful, I try to whisper in her ear, but mostly just blow on her neck. She laughs and I wonder if I've tickled her.

There you go again, she says, and takes another hit.

That's not odd, I say, I mean it. I work one hand up her thigh and carefully place the other hand at the top of her skirt. She has a smooth lower stomach. I pull back the hand on her thigh to keep my balance.

Don't fall off the bed, she says, smoking and tapping her bare foot on the carpet.

I push my fingers underneath her panties. You think you'll ever have children?

No, she says, I don't want them.

My fingers slip into the curls of her pubic hair and what I feel down there is something I haven't felt before, like a seam on a baseball.

Oh, I say, pulling my hand out. It's true.

Emily is startled. What? she says, standing. Her skirt is crooked.

So you did have an abortion?

What are you talking about?

There's a seam.

A what?

You can tell me. It doesn't matter. I'm starting to really like you. I want you to trust me with things. I'm sorry I startled you. I'll tell you something about myself: I don't know how to ride a bike. Isn't that funny?

The joint burns close to her fingers. Her hazel eyes

narrow.

Look, I just heard a stupid rumor from some kids and it has been on my mind. I'll leave, I'm sorry. I mean this and am prepared to go. I feel spent and ashamed for behaving as such. There is the issue with Bud and Nadine, too. I don't know anything about their love, I didn't even know he could speak. I can't remember exactly what the Scarecrow's problem was in *The Wizard of Oz*. Was he missing a heart?

Not that it's any of your business, but I miscarried last year.

Oh. What about the seam down there?

You aren't very experienced are you?

I approach her cautiously and remove the joint from her fingers. I drop it in the lemonade, it extinguishes with a hiss. She lets me take her hand. I guess it's pretty obvious, huh?

She nods her head, eyes on my face, mouth tight, shoulders tensed.

I want to start over, I say. She lets me lead her back to the bed where she sits down. I'm sorry you lost your child.

I didn't want it anyway.

You've been hurt, I can see that.

No shit.

Lie down.

She does, reluctantly, on her stomach. I massage her shoulders but they do not yield. I let my fingers follow her spine and smooth out her skirt. Lightly tracing down the back of her legs, I take her feet in my hands. I hold them as if they were blown glass.

What are you doing? she asks, rising up on her elbows.

Everything's going to be fine, I tell her. She laughs at this and shakes her head.

I look out the window and try to picture myself in the lawn, at night, peeping. The me now seeing the me then. With my eyes there I work desperately on her callused feet until they soften.

Horseshoes

Bud and Nadine are by the grill on the patio. A minister pronounced them husband and wife at the Baptist church a few hours ago and this barbecue is their reception. A neighbor ordered a champagne fountain but it hasn't arrived. She, the neighbor, couldn't make it herself. Emily and I are tossing horseshoes. I loosened my tie but Bud hasn't yet. He must be uncomfortably hot over the coals; he's cherishing the day, believing himself dapper in his little rented tuxedo. Hell, he does look good, I suppose. Nadine has a new white dress with chiffon and lace. A *Whisper of lace*, as Emily pointed out to me earlier when I asked what that shiny stuff was. Emily has been wonderful. She dressed Nadine and applied the makeup, wheeled her down the aisle right on cue. I stood next to Bud and swatted him when he got too fidgety. Then the vows. Bud said I do in his sing-song voice and Nadine, with great effort, mouthed I do when asked. She doesn't speak after the stroke. I don't know if a marriage is official if you don't say the words. She could have been saying, I'm through or Not true and nobody'd know. The truth is, you could see she meant forever in her face.

Those blue eyes said it clearly enough.

Summertime insects collide against the house with soft thuds. There are katydid husks on the trees outlining our property. Emily and I are down here next to the tomato garden. She's up a ring or two. I am in love with her, absolutely. First I fell in love with her mom, Ms. Hunter, she's dynamite, but I'm thinking now that was lust. With Emily I laugh all the time. Her minty breath lingers on my clothes in a way that makes me feel cleaner than I've ever felt before. She has suffered through bad relationships and is bright enough to know I'm the real thing. I'm gentle with her, I don't believe I'll ever make her cry.

Bud is standing on a cinder block so he can flip the burgers. He is too short to turn the patties without help. Nadine is smiling with her hands folded in her lap. The wedding ring looks super-gold against her white dress, her frail fingers, in the afternoon sunlight. Bud will be a spectacular husband, I believe now. The two of them are awkward, there's no doubt. Nadine has these spasms and throws her food across the room if she doesn't have a tight grip on her plate, and people think Bud's a midget. At first, I was overprotective of my mother. I didn't want to see her hurt again. Besides, I had committed myself to taking care of her. Then I discovered Emily. Somehow she helped me come to terms with the fact that Nadine and Bud needed me but wanted each other.

At the reception I told Bud I was proud of him and his eyes welled up with tears. He tried to choke them back. Then I told him that maybe once and a while I'd refer to him as Dad, and he wept like a child. I hugged him and he tried to throw his arms around my waist, which didn't work. He fastened his thumbs to the belt-loops in my slacks and gave me a squeeze. I nearly got mushy myself.

I've found money in the stock market, enough to support us with the insurance Nadine gets from the accident and Bud's exterminator paychecks. The market is a cinch, newspapers tell you everything. I know when to hold em and when to fold em. I've earned enough to buy Emily dresses and lingerie. We've made love, I'm getting better at it. I've learned to pace myself by breathing slowly. The world is fine. Hell, I think everybody's happy. There's a summer breeze and I'm not sweating in this heat with my suit on. Emily kisses the back of my neck and tells me that it's my turn. She has a silver dress that breaks just above her knees with a slit moving up her leg exposing thigh when she leans forward.

Yeah, it sure is my turn, I'll take it.

I look at the railroad spike sticking out of the lawn, swing my arm back, and release the horseshoe. It starts to climb, wavering slightly. Then the wind carries a smell I know immediately. Pabst Blue Ribbon and sweat. It is my father's scent.

He is standing in the side-yard, neither in the back nor in the front of the house. Nadine and Bud cannot see him from their position on the patio. I have not seen him in ten years or more, ever since I was eight. There is a cleft in his chin I don't remember. The one picture I have of him, one he sent for my sixteenth birthday, one I've studied and kept in a small teak frame in my room, didn't show him with a cleft in his chin. In the picture he has on a Cubs baseball cap that casts shadows over most of his face, blurring the details. He's wearing faded-gray overalls and it occurred to me that he might be a farmer. I didn't know what he did, at sixteen. Nadine told me as far as she knew he was a salesman.

Sold tractors? I'd asked.

No, bits and pieces of anything. He won sales awards selling fishing gear, I know that, Nadine said. He mentioned that.

Why didn't I get any gear for my birthday? I don't fish, but I'd have tried back then knowing the hooks were from him.

Now he is wearing a tan blazer and off-white corduroy slacks. The brown tie around his neck is too small; there's a grease stain on his left knee. He's got a gut and is nearly bald, his head is glistening in the balm. Still, he's handsome, perhaps the casual way his shoulders are thrown back and his feet planted to the ground. The stance says, *I'm here for you, come on.* At the same time it says, *I could give a shit about any of this.*

The horseshoe is ascending. My old man has a package in his hand wrapped in blue-and-white paper with champagne glasses floating around. Is it a wedding gift? What could my father possibly give Nadine now? He has not provided for her. Child support was a joke. I dropped out of school and found a job at a deli, then an animal hospital, a chicken restaurant, paper boy, pharmaceutical-runner; whatever I could fit around Nadine. I introduced her to Bud. The package doesn't look heavy in his hand. Wine glasses? Silverware? A tackle box? I think that's a wasp buzzing around his elbow. His eyes are gray-green and watery and the expression in his mouth tells me he is recollecting things; processing me, his son.

Taller than me, he thinks. *Thin, too thin, really, he'll need to broaden that chest before anyone takes him seriously. He's still got his hair, that's what mine looked like at his age, I'll need to tell him to forget about it, it'll never last.*

At eight, I remember my father taking me down to Byrd park, to the quarry where we sat on weathered stones and floated soda-can ships and Styrofoam sailboats with sipping-straw masts. He packed bologna sandwiches, mine without crusts and lettuce, his with extra mayonnaise. We talked about how ducks were the strangest animals in the park. We tossed rocks at our boats until they sank or sailed out of range. After a while he told me he would be leaving and to be a big boy about it. What I thought he meant was that he was going to the store for ice cream, or driving up to Langdon to see his father, grandpa, for the weekend, he did that sometimes, or over to Tritch's to fetch fresh ears of corn to go with supper. I said OK and found a friend on the swing-set. He left. I don't have any memory of his back fading into the twilight or of him saying *I love you, son* or any sharp pain he was trying to choke back that showed in his eyes. I was swinging, happily. I never thought he meant forever. A few weeks later I figured it out. Nadine gave me reasons I didn't buy.

The horseshoe is still rising. It is rusted at its base. I have flecks of reddish steel under my fingernails. The smell of cut-grass mingles with my father's scent. I hear the whack of a wooden baseball bat against a ball somewhere up the block. The sound makes my teeth ache. Have those crickets been humming this loud all along?

At twelve, after Nadine explained that my father was an alcoholic who ran off with a waitress, I gave her the silent treatment for nearly a year. My father wasn't the man Nadine thought he was. Once Dad took me for a drive in the country. We weren't going anywhere, just listening to music. A song came on that he told me to remember. It was April and dragonflies were everywhere. They zipped past the car. One fat fly smashed itself on the windshield. We both said, ouch. Then he said, *He won't have the guts to do that again!* I laughed and laughed. I tried to explain this to Nadine. She didn't think anything was funny. I refused to speak to her until I was thirteen when I accidentally asked her to pass the Fruities at breakfast. She passed them and wept. There was no reason for her to cry. I suppose I was becoming a man. I apologized. She'd suffered, obviously, no need to blame her. I wanted to get to the bottom of things. I wrote letters to my father: *Remember the time we flew a kite out in the Field when there was no wind. You said it flew on Lindwall willpower. Remember that?* And, *Dad, I was trying to think of the title to that song you told me never to forget. Why did you want me to never forget it? Did you know you were leaving then? Didn't it go, "The leader of the band is tired and his eyes are growing old. But his blood runs through my instrument and his song is in my soul," isn't that how it went?* I sent a half-dozen unanswered letters to return addresses on child-support checks he occasionally sent: Akron, Omaha, Jefferson City, Louisville, Cicero, Kankakee. Then I turned sixteen and got the picture. The return address was in a town called Bunny, Arizona. I figured I'd visit, took on night work at the morgue making sure nothing moved, earned half the money it took to buy an airline ticket out west, and Nadine had her stroke.

My father's face is framed in the up-turned horseshoe as it has found its peak and is heading down, spilling bad luck on him. Above a flock of blackbirds are passing. Their cries sound like hangers on racks of clothes at JCPenney's as undecided customers check out shirts, skirts, slacks, bathing-suits; not this one, not this one, not this one...

My father is thinking that there is still time to get to know me. I'm sure there's regret. He will ask for my forgiveness and if it were as simple as that I'd give it to him right off the bat. *I forgive you, no big deal, I'm not hurt anymore. Let's have a drink.* He'll try to understand how I've been. *What do you want to know? I can't tell you everything, you've been gone so long; nearly forever. It's like when you read a book and learn about a character for a few hundred pages. You put the book down and forget. I could be your Willy Wonka. Or was it Charlie working at the chocolate factory? What's that, you didn't read it? I'll bet you did, just don't remember now. What about Ishmael, remember him? Oh come on, you fish, you've got to know Ishmael. He never got seasick like I got the time Mom and I went on that cruise in Vero Beach. Yeah, I've been to Florida. Wanted to go to Disney but there wasn't time. Want to know why? Which moment do you want, Dad?*

Anything. What's new?

Hey, I finally learned how to ride a bike!

Yeah, good for you, son, I'm proud of you. I always had the darndest time getting you to straighten it out. You didn't want to let go of those training wheels.

I guess. Well, I learned now. You tried to teach me?

Yeah, I bought you that green dirt-bike with the frog-sticker on it.

No, no frog sticker. That waitress have a son?

What's your mother been telling you? Remember I'm still your father. A green frog, big smile. On the handle-bars.

Whatever. Mrs. Barton taught me. Remember Joan?

Of course I remember Joan.

Of course he would remember Joan. She enlightened

my mother, I've come to find out. Tried to nudge Nadine and Edward into couple's therapy. When things turned to shit Mrs. Barton shouldered my mother's insecurities and gave Nadine a little spine of her own. Then AA. That could have been the breaking point for him.

I bought a ten speed.

Great. Maybe we could ride down to the quarry. I'll buy you a Dairy Queen.

Quarry's gone, Dad.

Oh.

It's a bank now.

Son, I'm trying here.

I know Dad.

What about with the ladies, you got that Lindwall-mojo working?

Mojo?

That charisma, that charm, that groove, you know.

Sure I do. Sure I've got it.

Your friend is quite a looker.

Don't look, Dad.

Perhaps he'd nudge my chin or pat me on the back or wink at me or say, *You know son, you've got to be careful about diseases…*or go inside the house that once held his life, into the kitchen he'd not remember like this, *There's something different in here… Are the doorframes wider somehow?* he'd think the space was unnecessary and maybe, finally when he realized, *Oh, right, they need to be extended so Nadine can wheel herself in and fix a bite,* maybe he'd feel a bit guilty about something, the excess fat in his own legs; anything. He'd palm a couple PBR's for us to drink out in the sunset-soaked lawn and catch up and catch up and catch up.

The horseshoe is dropping and I'm starting to think

that it might have been a bad throw. What can I say, I was distracted.

Dad, I can do better.

I'll ask him where he has been, not because he owes me explanations, I'm beyond that now, I just missed him, missed who he could have been.

I've been working.

Doing what?

Sales mostly. I'm good at it. People trust me. When that doesn't pay the bills I do carpentry, mining, laying railroad tracks, lawn mower; anything.

Swell.

Boy, I can still bend you over a knee if you keep patronizing me.

This after cocktails, after catching up.

I'm not.

Leaving your mother was the hardest thing I've ever done and leaving you was no picnic either. You can't understand this, but it's like I woke up one day and realized I had the perfect wife, a wonderful boy, a house, respect on the job, everything I'd always thought I wanted. That frightened me.

Then I'd wonder if he was drunk. Would he preach to me this way if he hadn't been drinking? *Do you believe this shit when you're sober?* I'd want to ask, but wouldn't. After all, here he is, on stage, finally. *Didn't that song that I've tried to forget that you told me to remember say, "I'm just a living legacy to the leader of the band?"*

You remember, huh? Son, I panicked, had to flee. Your mother was better off without me then.

That song was about a father and son who were musicians. When the old man kicked it, the son played on out of love and respect for his Dad. How does that relate to us?

I don't know. It was just a sad song. I thought you should hear it. The music isn't always so good, son. The sweet song doesn't play forever. When it sours, my advice to you is to work. Get up in the morning, shake out your oats, square yourself up to the day. Day by day.

That's what you've done?

Yes, sir, I have. You'll do it to.

I'm interested in the stock market.

What for?

Money, support Mom. She can't do much, you know?

That's too bad. I'll have to talk to her, try to cheer her up.

She doesn't talk. I can't explain to you how she communicates. Ask Bud.

Horseshoe is plummeting. Mrs. Barton was the neighbor who ordered the champagne fountain. Maybe my father is delivering it? What coincidence, really, the old man is back in town working for the discount liquor store up on Kinzer Ave. I've been there a few times and never seen him. That's about perfect. Wonder how long he's been in town? Did it slip his mind that this was once his house? What's he going to do now? He knows I've seen him, his lip is twitching.

He'll ask where he should put the fountain.

Set it up there, on the patio. Thanks. No, you know what, I think it'd look better in the center of the lawn where we can all see it, like the centerpiece. Sorry to bother you. Actually, how about you drop it down here by the tomatoes that way we can all enjoy the splendor of the garden this evening with a nice alcohol spray, toast this new marriage. Sounds good, doesn't it Pop? You could stay for a quick one, couldn't you? On second thought, why don't you take it down the block and stick it in one of Tritch's cornfields with the wasting scarecrow? There's nothing like a sunset in the field. Put it there, Edward, we'll join you when the sun's ready. How about that? There'll be a tip in it for you, old man. Here it is: You've screwed us once, alcoholic, all you can do now is work yourself into oblivion; sell doorknobs or whatever someplace else. You can keep whatever change is left. I could say this. I might say this after horseshoes, god-damnit.

The horseshoe is starting to topple end over end as it descends.

The truth is that nothing my father does now will ever erase what he has already done. So be it. Let's not talk about the past. Let me look at you, see your smile. I've heard that I have your teeth, *Let me see your teeth, Dad.*

The horseshoe is way too far to the left. A terrible throw. Emily will beat me. How can I introduce my father to her? I don't want her to meet him.

Maybe that's not my father in the side-yard standing with the package. It's been so long. There could be some sort of spigot wrapped up nicely for looks. He might be a delivery man. This could be his uniform. I've never worked at a liquor joint, but if I did, I'd probably smell like this man, like my father too.

The horseshoe flops to the ground several feet away from the railroad spike. The man moves toward the patio. Two workers appear hefting the champagne fountain.

Nice try, Emily says, placing her hand on my shoulder.

She is patronizing me. I don't mind.

Thanks, I'll do better, I say, slipping my hands into my pockets.

Emily tosses her hair and prepares to throw her horseshoe. I measure my steps carefully in the lawn as I walk toward the house to introduce myself.

Milkweed

I sold most of my peanuts to a group of thinly bearded men before I loosened my tie and locked up to arm wrestle a man who may have been Jesus. I felt obligated, they were paying customers. Plus they taunted me because I limp some. They don't know anything, though, I've spent some time in a wheelchair, my arms have been worked out.

One of the men, maybe Moses, calls the bets and Jesus yanks my arm half to the table. It takes me a second to recover and stabilize. Jesus doesn't look strong, got arms like bamboo, but when he leans into you it's tough to fight him off.

I am losing, and he isn't struggling. I remember an old-timer back in Kentucky, toothpicklike, arm wrestle a giant farmer and win by making quick jerking movements with his wrist. I try this and it works. Jesus is pinned.

The men want another match, this time Southpaw-style, but I won't bite. I'll just be leaving, I say, and make my way to the door. Moses escorts me carrying the briefcase I use to carry peanuts.

At the door he hands me a flowered handkerchief.

He says, I do believe you're dripping, sir.

I take the hanky and dab at my neck. When I offer it back he refuses. I stuff it in my shirt pocket.

I didn't have my money on you, he says, handing me a stack of bills.

Well, I reply, and reach for my briefcase. He doesn't let me have it.

You've got nice arms.

Thanks.

His nose, up close, is enormous.

The others and I have taken the liberty to expand your career by adding some books to your case, sir. What's your name again?

Deet. Books?

The distributing type. You distribute don't you?

Sure, yeah, peanuts, that's my job.

We bought most of your peanuts.

Look, I just got back here. The peanut manager's a reasonable man. The thing to do is work myself up to cashews or macadamia nuts. Those nuts sell big.

Try pushing books.

I'm thinking maybe this is some scam, something self-help. I've done dictionaries. That was no good.

We're talking Bibles here, the word of our Lord, and when he says this his voice is curt and loud.

They won't sell.

Don't charge too much.

No thanks.

You keep the profits, all of them. We're not asking for anything from you. Just sing the song of the Lord.

I've got a rotten voice.

You know the Lord?

No.

Before I can react Moses jerks his hand around and smacks me on the forehead with his palm. Think, boy.

I do. I don't appreciate being called a boy; it's a term I cannot seem to outgrow. I know he doesn't mean it to denote age, it's more of a Southern-thing, though we aren't south, but it stings all the same. I don't look boyish. I've got crooked teeth which never let me smile and the little hair I have is starting to gray. I'm working on a beer gut because I'm under the impression women like a bit of fluff. As for God, I don't know. I suppose I owe Him for giving me life. God or Ray. Ray's the mutt who encouraged me to walk again. He demanded I get up and play, which, I did eventually. Then we went door-to-door and I tried to sell the dog, sort of. Nobody bought Ray, I figured they wouldn't, it was more performance than anything else, he had a slight touch of mange, people paid me to go away. We worked well together. Then Ray had an accident with a skunk in Tennessee. Whimpering and whining he found me where I'd sheltered in a cemetery, the best place to crash, I believe. He had that skunk-stink and wanted some sympathy. I hesitated. He noticed; cast his eyes at me like I'd struck him. Then I said, Come on, embraced him, and got skunky myself. In the morning he was gone. He left a pile of shit by my head. I don't blame him. I had that moment of doubt, plain and simple. That was a good dog. I guess the difference between Ray and God is that God's still around. Where else does He have to go?

Yeah, I say softly to Moses, I suppose I owe the Lord.

Hallelujah.

Hallelujah, Amen.

Now you've got it.

Do I go door-to-door?

Find yourself a pulpit. Preach the word of our Lord.

I'll do what I can, I assure him uncertainly.

He stands there smirking, scratching his hand on his pant leg.

I take the briefcase. It is heavy, heavier than peanuts. I notice that Jesus has been watching us from the arm-wrestling table with his gray eyes, a thin trail of smoke drifts from his cigarette, his head is half-cocked. I salute him with the bills. He mutters something I cannot hear. Moses places his hand on my back and I am in the street.

At a bench I wait for a bus and open the case. I leaf through one of the Bibles without reading any words. My old man had a Good Book which buckled together with a leather strap. He carried that thing with him everywhere, like it was a god-damned lung. Never once saw him open it.

It occurs to me I might have better luck with women lugging around a bunch of Bibles. Women read. Back south when I sold dictionaries I met a belle who taught me everything I know about language. Especially love and fear. Things are different here in the Midwest. It's tough to meet ladies door-to-door with peanuts. I did once, then I decided to stick to bars. Women aren't dangerous with a drink in their hand. They aren't confused. They either want peanuts or they don't.

A man across the street is running in full stride, his off-red tie scissoring in front of his chest, his Johnston and Murphy's kicking high and scuffing the sidewalk. I've got similar shoes. I don't know why he's running and a bus slides between us before I can figure it out.

I hold my breath as I bake in the fumes waiting for the door to open, then board.

A woman sitting across from me has a fish bowl in her lap. She has fine legs, probably does aerobics. The fish in the bowl may be dead. It is just hovering in the middle as water laps dangerously around the top, threatening to spill out onto her nice white skirt. Heavy lipstick makes her appear to be smiling although she is not, probably because her fish is dead. I can see where makeup runs into her bleached hairline.

I lean forward and say, I'm sorry about your fish.

She doesn't seem to have heard me. I don't know if it is from the motion of the bus or her cleavage, but I am getting an erection. I tent my hands awkwardly over my genitalia and hope it goes down.

There is a smudge on my window where someone had rested their sweaty or greasy head. The sun can't filter through smudges like this one and I do what I can in my condition to scoot away from the window.

The bus stops, I am at full mast. A man with an obvious toupee gets on and drops next to me in the half-seat. He doesn't need to do this. There are a million empty places. As the bus moves forward he crosses his legs as if to purposely expose his red socks pulled partially over his sickly white legs, perhaps for me to inspect. I don't.

So, the man says in a nasal-voice, where are you going today?

I ignore him and try to will my erection down. I'm thinking of moving back over to the smudged window. The woman in makeup sneezes into her hand. The fish bowl jiggles. I can't believe the water doesn't spill.

God bless you, I say.

That was a cough, she says, I didn't sneeze.

Oh. I pause for a moment and say, Sorry about your fish.

What? she asks.

The man sitting next to me snakes out his hand, brushes my erection and disrupts my makeshift tent, and clutches my wrist. He leans over and whispers to me, his breath foul, She's not your type.

What? I ask.

I asked you that, the woman says.

Oh, no, I wasn't talking to you. The fish, I'm sorry about your fish. I'm sorry that it died. I try to move away from the man.

She likes to float like this, the woman says quietly. She glances around the bus at the open seats. I wouldn't keep her if she was dead.

Ha! the man next to me says, his hand tight on my wrist. I can feel your pulse! I can feel your heart beating. He digs into my skin with short fingernails and begins to drum his free hand against his leg.

The woman is trying to frown in her lipstick. The fish, a yellow fish, blows an air bubble. The man squeezes my wrist and stares at the side of my face. If I had it in me I'd punch him in the mouth. Instead, I concentrate on unpleasant thoughts in order to collapse my erection. I think the man wants to put his head on my shoulder. The woman is leaning into her window. I feel miles from the blurry buildings falling away outside. To relax, I hold my breath and count, *one, two, three*—the week I spent in jail, before cops figured everything out, I struggled out of my wheelchair and onto the toilet where everyone could see me and taunt—*four, five, six*.

The bus stops, I untangle myself, softer now, and exit, briefcase in tow. I don't turn around. On my wrist I see a row of purple bruises which look like bite marks.

The street winds up a hill tiredly, cars brake and pant. A boy by a streetlight whispers, Papers, thirty-five cents, over and over again. I tell him that he needs to speak louder, put some spirit into the sale. With a slight lisp he mentions that I should mind my own damned business.

I'm not sure what my business is with these Bibles. As it happens, God set a bar at the top of the hill. I still have a jar or two of peanuts, I thank Him. I try to cross myself but is just looks like I'm swatting at gnats, and I enter.

When you're sitting at a stool pruning your glass-drinking hand with a series of drinks that drown your cocktail napkin in a joint called *Baby Hannah's*, so a sign on the wall indicates, and everything starts to seem all right in measurable gulps, you feel inclined to talk to the old souse bastard a few stools down and eye the suburban housefly at the other end of the bar half-smoking, standing with something fruity in a tall glass.

The drunk a few stools down says his name is Gus. I introduce myself as Rudolph because I've never done that before. I say my name loud enough for the housefly to hear. She is smoking her cigarette with too much teeth. No matter, she is a beauty with long, straight brown hair falling to her hips. In times past I'd say that she's the type that doesn't belong here, in a bar, with a wedding ring, seeking comfort. But now, hell, there she is, waiting for something to happen like the rest of us. I talk to Gus in order to draw the housefly's attention. She's the eavesdropping type.

Know much about the Bible?

Gus does not, he has one though, sort of; it opens

up with a little compartment inside made to hold a flask
of whiskey, and his old woman thinks he's honest on
Sundays. Gus is wrinkled and bleak in the sense that a
painter painting him might simply make a swash of gray
and be finished.

Peanuts? I ask.

Nah, he says, they do me no good. Do you have any
p'kin seeds?

Gus is drinking Old Crow, a drink that gives a man
bad breath. The housefly is listening but I dare not bring
her in yet. No.

Gus explains that he'd like to get a hold of some
pumpkin seeds because his old woman told him they
would help him get it up. I know what he means, I've
heard that about the seeds, I'd pester him about it, but
I have been engaged by a group of college students who
think they can out-drink me. One of them says he knows
me from down south in the papers. He asks if my name
is Deet, which it is, though not now, I've just introduced
myself as Rudolph, a nice name. Those things in the past
are irrelevant, I insist on being Rudolph. The boy doesn't
listen and explains to his friends that I got caught up in
a bizarre love affair with a married woman who offed
her husband and realized she could blame me because I
had fallen on my head, lost my mind, and been stuck in
a wheelchair. The thing he says he doesn't understand is
how I recovered. I'm not prepared to get into that. Since
the other boys are interested, he mentions that the married woman's daughter bit a police officer on the cheek
when they tried to take her to a foster home. They had
to restrain her. He can't imagine anyone who'd want to
adopt that little bitch after what she'd done, she was like
the growling mutt at an animal shelter who gets stuck

with the needle first. The college boys laugh. I tell him that's not exactly right. He says he's glad I'm better and pats me on the back. They line up shots, I easily overturn them, they want me to tell them a story, I mention I've got some drinking to do at the bar, they drift back into the corner with smirks.

I gamble an uneasy grin at the housefly. She comments that I am quite a drinker and I shimmer a little. At this point it is critical not to offer a drink yet, may scare her off, besides, she's still got some in her glass. Asking for a cigarette may work, but I am urged to relieve myself and quietly get up.

In the bathroom I pass the urinals, pausing a moment to glance at a picture of a wave along the seashore. I cannot tell if the wave is advancing or receding, but it is not important, the picture is there to help reluctant urinators urinate. I've had problems at urinals before so I don't use them. I step into one of the three stalls. As I unzip, I notice an egg in the bottom of the toilet. It is brown, speckled, maybe laid by a frustrated hen. It seems to be peeping at me. This makes me uncomfortable. I start to leave the stall, try my luck in the next one, when the bathroom door opens and someone crosses over the sticky tile to the stall next to mine. I crouch and wait for him to do his business. He is not doing anything but breathing and this is slow and ragged. I wait. The faucet is leaking. I want to go to the bathroom but something in the air won't let me. I hold my breath and count, still bent slightly; *one, two, three*—a song I used to sing with angel Chauncy comes to mind, "Let's all sing like the birdies sing, tweet, tweet, tweet, tweet, tweet," I know that after this verse I'm supposed to whistle but my mouth is all tongue and I cannot—*four, five, six.*

A slip of toilet paper appears in my stall under a rattlesnake boot. I make out the word "SWEETY" scribbled poorly in red ink, quickly zip up, and rush for the door.

Back at the bar I try to settle myself with a drink. Gus is gone and I can't help wondering if he had been wearing boots. He didn't seem like the type. I refuse to approach the college students. The housefly has lit another cigarette. My drink is terrible and I notice a pubic hair coiled at the bottom of the glass. The hair does not disgust me as much as it frightens me; I don't know where it has been.

It is hot in here, isn't it? the housefly asks, stirring a new drink with a toothpick umbrella. She has taken the wedding ring off, I think, maybe she didn't have it in the first place.

I'm not sure what she means.

You're perspiring, she says trying to make her voice husky and seductive.

I take the handkerchief Moses had given me earlier and wipe my brow with it. The bar is swallowing me, I manage.

The housefly gulps her drink. Is that story true? You were in a wheelchair?

It would take years to explain properly, I say.

I want her to respond, *I have the time*, but she doesn't, she tosses her hair over a shoulder. A girl I knew in elementary, Lindsey Sharp, had hair like this which almost touched the back of her knees. Us boys gave her a hard time because all she used to do at recess was comb, comb, comb.

I'm going outside, I say, taking out money, perhaps you'd like to follow me. I place the bills amongst the cocktail-napkin flotsam on the bar and push them toward her, wanting to pay her tab. I cannot say for certain, but I think she knows what I'm trying to do. She hasn't blinked in a while and her cigarette is low.

I try not to hurry out of the bar and I don't check people's feet for rattlesnake boots. I still need to pee but there is no way I'm using the bathroom here.

Outside it is not quite twilight. The paper boy is gone and there aren't any cars to speak of on the street. There should be, it is rush-hour-time but for some reason things are quiet. The silence makes me tired. Tired of walking around. I could use a desk job. I don't have what it takes to be an alcoholic. I don't have the stamina. And bar-people, I'm having doubts about them. Drinkers are always trying to convince you of something crucial and immediate.

There is an alley I enter and realize that I've stepped in salt water taffy and my right shoe is a mess. I hobble along. The alley opens up into an old playground surrounded mostly by buildings. There's a swing-set without a swing, monkey bars, and a slide. A knotted tree leaning against a broken fence shakes a little rain from its leaves, rain I do not remember. I pee in the corner which is all I've wanted for so long.

When I'm empty again, I make my way to a rusty slide with two missing rungs on the ladder and climb. At the top I sit. I will wait for the housefly. I pick at the taffy with the longest fingernail I have and my thumb. A pool of stale water has gathered at the bottom of the slide. By squinting I can see mosquitoes mating, I think, they could be eating each other. I imagine mosquitoes are cannibalistic, they're bloodsuckers, someone's always got to have more blood.

The sun is somewhere behind me and my shadow,

down in front, is twitching as it juts out across a thicket of milkweed pushing up from the pinched concrete in an old hop-scotch pattern. That damned determined weed. When we were kids my friends and I ripped the plants up so the sap ran free and threw milkweed grenades at each other during recess. I remember a friend of mine, Thomas, approaching Lindsey by the merry-go-round and kindly asking if he could help comb her hair. I'll never know the struggle she went through in that moment trying to decide if she should trust Thomas. I couldn't tell you if she regretted that decision for the rest of her short life. She could have been questioning that instant, when she hesitantly handed the big blue brush to Thomas and cautiously turned around, the night she drowned in the quarry five years later. They say weeds tangled her ankles, held her down. She was with her sister who called out forever but there was no reply. They found her because the tip of her hair floated up and barely broke the surface of the water. I don't know what she was thinking then. She trusted Thomas, perhaps she remembered that he had been mistreated when we were younger. She didn't see him wave me forward from my hiding place behind the tunnel-slide, armed. I nailed her with the milkweed. Thomas dropped the brush in the dirt and we took off like rabbits. When Lindsey tried to get the stuff from her hair she just complicated the matter and the Teach ended up having to cut it out with inefficient scissors from Art Class. I felt badly, of course, I didn't know what damages it would cause. I feel worse about it now knowing that she had to live with short hair when she wanted long hair again and that when it finally did return to its original length, she would die. The hair was growing, marking her days, and I'm the one who overturned the hour-glass. Mr. Sprinkle, the principal who held a vendetta, paddled me roughly until my ass stung. My third-grade teacher made me write five hundred sentences—*I will not throw things at girls or else I'll suffer the consequences.* I didn't know what the word *consequences* meant, but I do now.

The taffy isn't coming off my Johnston and Murphy's. I take the sticky shoe off and rub it against an edge on the slide. Steam is coming out of a Laundromat next door. On the other side of the fence I see a chicken pen. They are so quiet in there.

I hear soft footsteps coming from the alley and think of the housefly. But it isn't Her. It is a slim man with a runny nose carrying my briefcase. He's wearing some sort of wrestling shoes.

Excuse me, is this yours?

Yeah. I hadn't noticed it was gone.

It must not be important.

Actually, no. Keep it. Well, give me the jar or two of peanuts, but the rest is yours. It's full of Bibles.

I'm not religious.

He sets the briefcase on the ground next to the slide and regards the bottom of his shoe.

I stepped in something, too, he says.

I bang my shoes together. They stick and separate.

That isn't going to help, he says.

What will?

We need something else sticky to counter it. I could take mine off and we could try rubbing them together?

I don't like that idea one bit. I put my shoe back on.

That milkweed there is pretty sticky, I say.

He looks at the concrete for a long time. Finally, he says, I'll bet it is. We could give it a try.

I climb down from the slide and approach the milk-weed, but he stops me before I can root it up.

Let's just stomp on it, he says. We'll play a game of hop-scotch together.

I don't remember how to play.

Neither do I.

I guess we could try it.

The man steps over to me and tries to put his arm around my shoulders. I hand him the handkerchief Moses gave me earlier. He dabs his nose and offers it back, I refuse and he stuffs it in his shirt pocket. I put my arm around him.

Lift a foot, he says.

I do. He does.

Now jump. With me.

We hop into the first square. Then we put our feet down for the second, and then forward; *one, two, one, one, two,* and we are on the other side. We spin and do it again. We trample the milkweed. It takes several turns before the stuff starts to come off the soles of our shoes.

Jason Ockert was born in Indiana, raised in Florida, and now resides in New York. In 1999, he won the *Atlantic Monthly* Fiction Contest, and in 2002 he received the Mary Roberts Rinehart National Fiction Award. Jason's stories have appeared in *McSweeney's, Black Warrior Review, Alaska Quarterly Review,* and elsewhere. He has recently completed a novel, *Passers-by,* and is working on a second collection of stories. Those are not his rabbit-hands on the cover.